Right from the beginning, Abram Noble felt very protective of Martha Lawford.

After a while he left, walking slowly back to the boardinghouse.

"You be sure to bring me your dirty clothes, Mr. Noble," Martha called.

"I will," he yelled back, waving. Before going inside the boardinghouse, he went around back to the corral to make sure his faithful mare, Charity, had plenty of hay and to give her her evening oats. He brushed and curried the rich bay horse. Stroking Charity's darker mane, he felt pride in the shiny plump animal. "I can't wait for you to see her, Charity," her murmured. "I hope you like her as good as I do." After a few more strokes with the brush, he put her in her comfortable stall in the stable and hurried to his own room and bed.

As he lay in bed, he thought about Miss Lawford again. His horse had more to eat and a better place to sleep than the girl and her dog. Somehow that didn't seem right.

But he smiled in the dark, remembering his visit. He had several things to do in the morning. Besides his own donation claim to check out, he had to find out about Miss Lawford's situation. And before he did that he'd better check around to see who needed clothes washed.

"Be with her, God, and protect her. You might be with me, too. I'd be thankin' You a long time if You'd help me get to know her better." He fell into a sound sleep.

VERALEE WIGGINS, author of many books, lives in Washington State with her husband. One of her novels, *Llama Lady*, was voted favorite contemporary inspirational romance by *Heartsong Presents* club members.

Books by VeraLee Wiggins

HEARTSONG PRESENTS

HP17—Llama Lady
HP33—Sweet Shelter
HP76—Heartbreak Trail

Martha My Own

VeraLee Wiggins

A sequel to *Heartbreak Trail*

Heartsong Presents

For Michael and Julie.

May God bless you both forever.

I love you with all my heart,

But He loves you much much more.

ISBN 1-55748-517-8

MARTHA MY OWN

Sporadic tears dampened Martha Ann Lawford's cheeks as she gazed east while leaning against the corner of her covered wagon. The wagon, battered from its long trip west, huddled alone on the north side of a Nez Percé Indian trail.

Immediately before her, eight rough buildings lined the trail, four on each side, forming a sort of dusty street. Behind the buildings on either side, large and small native weeds grew among the drying grass across the prairie. Several dirty light-colored tepees marred the view north of the street, and the three or four shacks on the south did little to improve the view. The few trees in evidence bordered the several rivers and creeks that flowed into and through Steptoeville, Walla Walla Valley, Washington Territory, her new home.

The brilliant sun shining on the snow-capped Blue Mountains forced Martha to shut out the clutter of shacks before her and allowed her to feel better. Surely God had something good planned for her after the long horrible trip she'd just endured.

She shuddered, remembering the terror of crossing those innocent looking hills only ten days ago. They had dragged trees behind the wagons to keep them from careening down the steep hillsides and destroying the wagons and killing the oxen.

I trust You, Lord, but I don't understand why You let our trip west turn into such a disaster. She straightened her

5

shoulders. Keeping her mind and body busy might prevent her from dwelling on the tragedy that had left her alone in a strange place.

"Come on, Josie," she said to her dog, "let's stroll down the street and see what those shacks are." The eight buildings she referred to stood about a hundred feet apart and looked nothing like the fine homes and businesses she'd left in Missouri six long months ago. Some of the buildings were constructed of slab, some of logs. Others consisted of rough boards nailed together in a haphazard fashion. Some had glass windows but most of the windows were made from some translucent material Martha didn't recognize.

Josie, though her ribs and protruding backbone poked almost through her long, matted, black, gray, and white fur, jumped with excitement at the thought of a new adventure.

Martha stepped into the dusty street that snaked under the rickety buildings; there were no sidewalks. A small sign in front of the first building on the north side of the street invited one and all to come in to find warm food and lodging. "They mean people with money," she explained to Josie before noticing her mangy-looking dog tearing up and down the street, raising a large cloud of dust. "Josie!" she called. "You get back here. Now." The dog dropped her tail and scurried back to Martha.

Next they passed a saloon, quickly, for Martha didn't want to be seen near the place. Slowing a few feet past the odious building, she giggled. Who did she think might see her or care what she did in this nearly unpopulated place?

A sign on the next rough wooden building announced it to be a trader's oasis; the roughly painted sign on the small building after that read: RACKETT'S TIN SHOP.

Then she came to a small stream separating the street from a barracks type of place with many buildings. Martha stood at the edge of the creek wondering why the buildings were deserted and what they had been. Then her eyes dropped to the brook before her, gurgling praises to God as it rushed over the smooth rocks. It looked shallow and had two small islands in the middle. After a moment she crossed to the other side of the street to check out the four buildings on the south side: an unoccupied store of some kind, then Chapman and Shaffer's Meat Market, another saloon, and a general store. Two saloons seemed a bit much to Martha considering that the entire town consisted of only these eight shacks.

As she hurried past the second saloon, the front door opened and a wild looking, middle-aged man came pouring out, almost as if propelled by some unseen force, perchance the barkeep's boot? The man gathered himself together, slapped his worn hat back onto his matted gray hair, and started to leave. Then, noticing Martha, he stopped in midstride, a grin splitting his thin lips. His squinty eyes took her in from head to toes.

"Well, whadda we got here?" he asked. "I ain't seen you around, blue eyes. You b'long to someone?"

Suddenly frightened, Martha turned away, but before she could take the first step, his long fingers wound around her arm and jerked her back.

"Why'd a young thing like you walk away when I'm atalkin'?" he asked, his voice thick with alcohol. Before Martha could move, his other arm reached around her and she found her face within inches of the foul-smelling man's.

"Josie!" she yelled at the top of her voice, before noticing the dog halfway down the short street, rolling in the dust. "Help, Josie!" she screamed, knowing the man could haul her away before the dog reached her.

Suddenly, the saloon door crashed open again and a taller, younger man emerged almost as quickly as the first man had. "Stop, Abe," the older man hollered as a fist landed somewhere on his person. Raising his hands, he tapped the new arrival's chest in an ineffectual attempt at self-defense. "Stop!" he screamed as a fist slammed into his face. "You ain't got no call to do that." A moment later, Martha's assailant lay in the dust, rubbing the side of his face, a large bruise showing already, and blood running from his mouth.

Finally, Josie arrived barking wildly and growling deep in her throat. Perceiving the man still on his feet to be the enemy, she hit him hard in the chest with her front feet, knocking him backward into the dust beside Martha's would-be assailant. Hopping instantly to his feet, the man dusted off the back of his denim pants. Martha noticed how tall, muscular, and tanned he looked.

In spite of her fear, Martha couldn't hold back a tiny nervous giggle. "No, Josie," she said softly, "you're too late." The dog stood beside her and looked at the men, the fur on her spiny backbone standing erect, a deep growl still rumbling in her throat.

The man who'd administered the beating stood over the downed man. "You'd better get out of here, Slick, before I lose my temper," he said softly. "And if you ever bother a woman again, I'll make you wish you were dead." The tall man had a clean honest look about him but suddenly Martha felt afraid of everyone.

"I didn't mean no harm," the man, Slick, whined. "I was just tryin' to meet the lady." He scrambled to his feet, grabbed his hat again, and lurched off down the street, rubbing his face with one hand and his back with the other.

"Thank you, sir," Martha said, edging away from the

man. If she could get back to her wagon she'd be content to stay there the rest of the day. Maybe forever. What kind of a place had she been dropped into, anyway?

But the man stuck out a big brown paw. "I'm Abram Noble," he said. "Mighty glad to make your acquaintance. Sorry about that fellow. Luckily you won't find many like him around here." He kept the big hand out there forever.

Finally, she allowed him to shake her small hand for a fraction of a second before she withdrew it. "I'm Martha Lawford," she said in a husky voice. "I certainly do thank you, and I'll feel much obliged if there aren't any more around like him."

She turned and started back toward her wagon, only to hear his footsteps behind, then beside her. "Where are you staying, Miss Lawford?" he asked with a familiarity that frightened her all over again. Should she tell him? That wagon with the battered cloth top offered little in the way of protection.

"I'm staying near town," she answered, realizing they'd be at the wagon in minutes. Where could she go to lead him off the track?

He grinned, keeping almost in step with her. "Where near town?" he asked. "I hope you aren't camping alone on the bank of one of the rivers."

She stopped and held a hand to him again. She had to get rid of him now. "No, I'm not. I'm perfectly all right. Thanks for seeing me this far, Mr. Noble. I'll probably see you around town." She turned, lifted her skirt a little, and began striding northwest across the dried grass, away from her wagon, thinking that maybe he'd go back now and she could return to it.

But less than a minute later, he walked beside her again. "I have a bad feelin' about you," he said in an easy, friendly way. "Why don't you just show me where you're staying so I won't worry anymore?"

She liked the man's looks. His clear dark eyes, his thin straight nose, and square jaw, together with his heavy mop of light brown hair gave him an upright, honest, and pleasant looking appearance. She liked his voice, too, and his manner. But he sure knew how to stick—like oatmeal to a pan on an overheated fire. She raised her eyes to meet his and shrugged. "I don't seem to have a choice." She pointed to the covered wagon almost behind them now, and south. "That's my house," she said, turning toward it. They reached it almost immediately. Josie crawled under the wagon into the shade and lay there, watching the pair.

"You can't stay in this thing," Mr. Noble said, stretching his neck to look inside. "It don't offer any protection a'tall. Not from four-legged animals or two." He turned and pointed toward the buildings from which they'd just come. "I'm stayin' at Martin's Boardinghouse. You'd best get a room there, too."

She didn't have to tell him she didn't have money, did she?

After a moment he went on. "What you doing out here alone? Where's your people? And your oxen?"

Martha gave a long loud sigh. She hadn't realized it but she really needed to talk to someone. "Are you purely sure you want to hear?"

"I asked, didn't I?" He sat on the tongue of the wagon. "Let's get comfortable. I have a feeling it's not a pretty story."

"You're right, sir," Martha said, easing down to the makeshift seat. "My older brother, Jackson, got out of the army last year and, ever since, he's talked of nothing else but moving to Walla Walla Valley. Said it was like

the Garden of Eden. He wouldn't stop talking, so finally
our family decided to come. Mama's brother and his wife
and son decided to come, too. We planned to all come
together but my aunt and uncle had a last-minute delay in
collecting the money from their farm. We'd already sold
our place and all our stuff. Everything we owned was in
the wagon so we couldn't wait for them. We'd hoped
they'd catch up with us on the Oregon Trail. They should
be along within a week.

"Our family. . .my parents, two brothers, and I started
west last March with a wagon train from Missouri." She
shook her head, remembering. "It seems a long time ago,
and the trip was so hard." She raised her eyes to his. "I
can't tell you how awful that trip was. But my parents
made it almost here before they. . .," she took a deep breath,
willing herself not to break down in front of this stranger,
"died of cholera." She stopped and dropped her head.
*Why, Lord? I still love You and trust You. . .but why did
they have to die? I loved them so much. And needed them
desperately.* Raising her head resolutely, she continued.
"We ran out of food right after that and my oxen were so
worn-out we had to leave them at Fort Hall.

"One of the families had extra oxen so they pulled me
this far. They wanted me to go on with them but I have to
wait here for my aunt and uncle." Her eyes burned so she
shut them tight. "I have to wait for them, Mr. Noble," she
continued a moment later. "They're all the family I have
left. Finally, the Butler family gave me some flour and
left me here, but they took my baby brother, William.
Said I'd have all I could do to take care of myself until
my aunt and uncle come. We'll get him next summer."

Swallowing loudly, Martha closed her eyes tightly
again. She'd never felt so alone in her entire life. If
Josie would just come out from under the wagon, she'd

give her a big hug.

Martha straightened her shoulders and smiled at the man, Mr. Noble. When she met his gaze, his red-rimmed eyes looked almost ready to cry, too.

His Adam's apple jerked up and down. "I guess that's about what I expected. What about your other brother? He die, too?"

She shook her dark head. "When we left the oxen at Fort Hall, he decided to go back and make sure our aunt and uncle were all right." She shook her head again. "I wish he hadn't. I need him more than they do."

They sat together in silence, each deep in private thoughts. She wondered why she'd told this stranger all her troubles. Now he knew her total vulnerability.

Finally, he met her gaze. "You don't have any money, right?"

She nodded. "But I can work. Maybe I could work at the boardinghouse. I know how to clean, and I can cook a little."

He dropped his eyes. "That's another sad story. The man got hurt bad so his wife and four daughters run the place. I think they're pretty broke." He leaned forward, his elbows on his knees, his chin in his hands, thinking. "You don't happen to play the piano, do you?"

She laughed out loud. As if anyone in this little town would pay her for playing. "As a matter of fact, I do," she said. "Is someone at the boardinghouse looking for a pianist?"

He shook his light brown head. "No. But there are two saloons. I'll bet I could talk one of them into hiring you. You could wait tables when you aren't playing."

"Sorry, I don't set foot into saloons, Mr. Noble. Don't you know they're the devil's playground?"

two

Abram Noble enjoyed the feel of the cold water on his face and arms as he washed up for supper; it really brought a man to life. But he kept thinking of the girl at the covered wagon.

He continued thinking of her as he ate the steaming meal Mrs. Martin and her daughters had prepared. Potatoes fried with onions in bacon grease, boiled turnips, some kind of meat. Roast horse, he thought to himself, trying to chew it. Boiled cabbage, tea, and bread and butter finished out the meal. He'd been there only three days but twice they'd served various kinds of melons. He'd enjoyed that all right.

He hardly heard the other men laughing and talking about how the strange girl had affected his brain. True, he could hardly force his thoughts from her.

In his mind he saw her long dark hair braided into a crown too heavy for her nicely shaped head. Enormous bright blue eyes shone from her heart-shaped face with its ivory complexion. Average height, but small boned, she looked young, very young. All together, she made a picture that Abe couldn't get out of his mind for even five minutes. Too bad her dress and sunbonnet were so worn and faded; they were not the proper clothes for a girl like Miss Lawford.

What would become of her? He'd gladly rent a room for her but he could tell from their encounter that she'd never accept help. No telling what could happen to her out there alone.

When he finished supper, his feet hit the dusty path. Clearly visible from the boardinghouse, the wagon sat on the north side of the trail only about a hundred yards west.

Nearing the wagon he noticed the girl had a small fire going and some kind of pot over the low flames. "Hello, Miss Lawford," he called in order not to startle her with his sudden appearance. "Thought I'd better make sure you're all right before—"

Josie the dog interrupted, bursting from beneath the wagon and with the roar of a tornado. Abe, remembering his earlier encounter with the animal, jumped back and forgot what he'd intended to say and almost about Miss Lawford altogether.

"Josie, girl! Stop!" the young woman commanded. The dog quieted immediately but planted herself between Abe and her mistress.

Abe felt a letdown. Why couldn't the dog have slept through his visit?

The girl returned her attention to the pot on the fire. It looked like white dough in the bottom, almost like a pancake but not quite. She scraped the stuff from the bottom, turned it over, and took the pot off the fire.

She smiled at him. "I'd offer you a chair if I had one." Then she brightened. "I have two boxes that I can empty real easy and we can sit on them." She jumped up from her position beside the fire where she'd been sitting on her heels. "I'll be right back," she said, hopping lightly to the frame of the wagon and disappearing under its white canopy. She appeared a moment later and dropped the boxes gently to the ground, before jumping down behind them. "Sit down and relax, Mr. Noble. These are dynamite boxes we packed food in."

She returned the pot to the fire. "I have to finish cooking our supper because I don't have many buffalo chips left. When it's finished, I can talk for a while." As Abe watched, she poured another batch of the pasty stuff into the pot and watched it carefully until she scraped it loose from the bottom and turned it over. A few minutes later she took it out of the pot and put more in. Then she cooked two more from the remaining paste.

"There," she said, plopping onto one of the boxes. "We can eat later. It won't matter if they're cold."

"Would you mind telling me what you just cooked?" Abe asked.

Miss Lawford smiled and dipped her head a bit. "Why, Mr. Noble, haven't you seen trail bread? I make it from flour and water." She shrugged. "It's supposed to have other things in it but flour's all we have." Josie whined and tried to snoot Miss Lawford's hand toward the bread. The dog's pitiful cries made Abe's heart ache for the half-starved animal.

The frail girl shrugged and fed one of the breads to the dog who took it in one gulp. "Sorry," she said. "We each get only a couple of these twice a day and you can see Josie's eager."

"Is that all you got to eat?"

Miss Lawford nodded, her face turning an attractive pink. "We're mighty thankful to have that, Mr. Noble. Our food was completely gone. No one on the wagon train had much either, but they gave me enough flour to last a week. . .until my aunt and uncle come."

Abe felt almost sick to think of this lovely girl trying to care for herself and her dog. And both of them nearly starving. "I got a gun," he said. "I could get you some meat. Rabbits, or something."

She perked up a moment, then settled down. "Only if you have too much for yourself," she said. "I have a gun too, but I'm afraid to shoot it." Josie put her front feet into Miss Lawford's lap, who then got up and fed Josie another piece of trail bread. It disappeared pitifully fast. Then she gave the dog one more, leaving only one small piece.

"I have a plan," she told Abe, her delicate face showing excitement. "Why couldn't I do washing for the men in the boardinghouse? Or wherever they live. I could do it right on the banks of that little creek down past the buildings." She pointed east, down the street. "How are people getting their things washed now?"

Abe, only in town three days himself, hadn't given that problem a thought yet. He shook his head. "I'm not sure, but I'll find out. That would be hard work."

Her laugh sounded like birds singing. "I'm not afraid of hard work, Mr. Noble. I washed clothes for several of the people in the wagon train. I spent most of my Saturday afternoons washing clothes. It wasn't easy but it was something I could do to help. One person was sick, one old and weak, some didn't even have wagons." She sighed then pulled her shoulders back. "My only problem right now is that I don't have any tallow to make soap."

He laughed. "I can buy you some soap right there in that first building on the right. It's a general store and sells most anything a man needs."

She stiffened. "I couldn't let you do that, Mr. Noble. Josie and I aren't your responsibility."

That idea didn't sound half bad to Abe. Never had he met anyone who made him feel so responsible. But he had to be careful not to frighten her away. "Maybe I could loan you the soap and you could repay me or do some of my clothes for free. Would that work?"

"Yes. It sounds good. Thank you, Mr. Noble. You really are, aren't you?"

"I really am what?"

"Noble." They laughed together. When they finished, she cast a questioning glance his way. "You know all about me but I know nothing about you, sir. That hardly seems fair."

She wanted to know about him? She'd opened up enough to ask? Well, he'd best not keep the lady waiting! "I hail from Iowa and have two parents and two sisters. I been in the army for the last six years. Got sent west to fight the Indians and that's what I been doing. Me and my company chased some Indian tribes past here a couple times and I noticed what a right purty valley it was. I sure understand how your brother felt.

"I tried to file a donation claim several years ago but they weren't allowing settlers in yet because of the Indian wars. No matter where I went, I kept remembering this little valley where the rivers meet. Well, finally the army turned me loose and the government opened the valley to settlers, so here I am. I'm looking for a piece of land I can't live without, so I can put a claim on it."

A look of pure bliss crossed Miss Lawford's face. "That's exactly what I'd like to do, too," she said.

At first Abe felt excitement at the possibility of having her for a neighbor. Then he remembered a man had to be twenty-one years old to make a claim. This slip of a girl couldn't be a day over fifteen. He wasn't sure whether women could make claims, anyway. "How old are you?" he asked quietly.

"I'm seventeen," she replied. "How old are you, sir?"

He laughed. After all, fair was fair. "I'm an old man,"

he said. "I'll celebrate my twenty-fifth birthday in December."

She nodded. "And what do you plan to do with this claim you're getting?"

He thought a moment. "Well, farm it, I guess, and run some cattle. Maybe some sheep and a few chickens. Plant me some fruit trees. I guess that ought to about do it."

"Oh, Mr. Noble, it sounds heavenly. I'm going to do it, too. First, I have to earn some money washing clothes to buy food for Josie and me, then I'm going to get a donation claim, too. I really am."

As dusk began to drop her curtain over them, Abe noticed mosquitoes. "I hope you will, Miss Lawford, but for now, how about letting me lend you enough money to get a room in the boardinghouse? I don't want you out here. You got no protection a'tall."

A smile curved her lips. "What do you call the hurricane that met you, Mr. Noble? Josie would die to protect me. I'd better stay right here until my aunt and uncle come. It may not be a palace, but it's free."

"You heard about the Indians?"

Her face blanched and her right hand flew to her throat. "What about the Indians?"

He smiled. "I never heard about them hurting anyone, but they walk right into people's houses and demand food. Everyone I know's given them something to eat and they leave. They stink like nothing you've ever smelled because they smear fish fat all over them. They think it keeps 'em warm. They scare people a lot, but as far as I know they don't hurt anyone."

"Oh, but I don't have anything to feed them. I'm nearly out of flour, too. That's why I have to wash clothes."

He smiled grimly. "You'll give them something to eat,

Miss Lawford, even if it's your last bite." Seeing her dismay he tried to think of something with which to cheer her. "They probably won't come here anyway, seeing you don't have a proper house."

"I hope not. I really hope not, Mr. Noble. That would purely frighten me to death."

After a little while he left, walking slowly back to the boardinghouse.

"You be sure to bring me your dirty clothes, Mr. Noble," Martha called.

"I will," he yelled back, waving. Before going inside the boardinghouse, he went around back to the corral to make sure his faithful mare, Charity, had plenty of hay and to give her her evening oats. He brushed and curried the rich bay horse. Stroking Charity's darker mane, he felt pride in the shiny plump animal. "I can't wait for you to see her, Charity," he murmured. "I hope you like her as good as I do." After a few more strokes with the brush, he put her in her comfortable stall in the stable and hurried to his own room and bed.

As he lay in bed, he thought about Miss Lawford again. His horse had more to eat and a better place to sleep than the girl and her dog. Somehow that didn't seem right.

But he smiled in the dark, remembering his visit. He had several things to do in the morning. Besides his own donation claim to check out, he had to find out about Miss Lawford's situation. And before he did that he'd better check around to see who needed clothes washed.

"Be with her, God, and protect her. You might be with me, too. I'd be thankin' You a long time if You'd help me get to know her better." He fell into a sound sleep.

three

Martha watched Mr. Noble striding away from her wagon until he went around the boardinghouse and was out of sight. "Well," she told Josie. "I think he'll really help me get started washing clothes. Maybe I'll make enough to buy you all the food you need." She hugged the dog's big head. Josie returned the caress with two swipes of her tongue across Martha's cheek. "Just you wait," Martha continued. "Things'll soon be better. I promise." She turned to the cold trail bread. Knowing she needed the strength the bread offered, she had a hard time getting out her next words. "We'll start right now. I already gave you three of the breads, but you're still hungrier than I. Here, you can have half of this last one." The dog didn't wait for a second invitation but gobbled the offered food.

Martha sat back down on the box and tried to make her piece last as long as possible. She chewed each tiny bite thirty-two times as her mother had taught her, and tried to think about something besides the food. The only other thing she could think about was the washing she might have to do and the strength she would need to do it. She took another tiny bite. As she chewed, three men approached the wagon from the west. Where had they come from? The street and people were the other way. Even the tepees were east and north. Becoming uneasy, she wondered who they could be and what they wanted.

Then she recognized Indians! She sat with her heart in her throat, terrified. *Protect me, Father. Make them be friendly.* When a deep growl rumbled from inside Josie, she reached an arm around her faithful dog's neck.

They stopped within ten feet of Martha, stared into her eyes, and waited. An almost unbearable stench, arriving with the Indians, made Martha's stomach lurch. She didn't know what to say or do. Would they even understand her language?

The three walked over to the tiny fire, and looked into the empty pot. One of them began motions as if eating. "Food," he said. He seemed to be the oldest of the three and wore buckskins. Soft moccasins covered his feet. The other two wore white man's clothes, worn and dirty overalls with ragged long-sleeved shirts. But like the older man, they wore soft deerskin moccasins. Long, matted black hair hung down their backs.

The old Indian caught her attention again, then repeated his request for food. Or was it an order?

Mr. Noble had warned her they'd want food. But she had so little! What would she do when it was gone?

"Food!" the Indian said again. The three surrounded her as she sat on the box and Josie's rumble grew louder. Mr. Noble had told her to feed them even if it was her last bite.

"You be good, Josie," she warned the dog. Scrambling to her feet, her knees shaking, she tossed four more buffalo chips onto the fire, poured two cups of her precious flour into the bowl and added water. When thoroughly mixed, she dropped spoonfuls onto the bottom of the pot.

The Indians looked friendlier as they watched her fixing the trail bread. They said something to each other then they all sat down beside the box she'd abandoned.

After turning the bread twice, she scooped it from the pot, cooled it a moment, and handed each Indian a piece.

They nodded deeply, saying something unintelligible. "You're welcome," she said, smiling. This wasn't nearly as bad as she'd feared—except she could ill afford losing the flour.

As each man took a bite, his expression changed to surprise then anger. All three jumped to their feet and started saying something to Martha at the same time. It didn't take her long to decide they didn't like the trail bread and wanted something else—now!

"I don't have anything else," she said, knowing they wouldn't understand her. "That's all my dog and I have to eat," she went on.

They caught the word "dog" and one of them gestured toward Josie, making motions of eating again. Martha dropped to her knees, reaching her arms around her friend. "No, no," she said. She kissed Josie's dusty face. "I love my dog. I'd never eat her."

After a few moments of talking together, the Indians tossed the trail bread to Josie, who wolfed it down. Then they left without another word. Martha watched them, wondering to which tepee they'd go, but soon they became specks on the western horizon. She dropped to the box, breathing hard.

She started laughing with relief, then couldn't stop. Realizing she'd become hysterical, she forced herself to take deep breaths until she regained control. Then she thought about their rejection of her food and used all her willpower not to start laughing again. "Well, Josie, at least they won't be back to bother us anymore. That's something, isn't it?" Their terrible stink still lingered heavily in the air so she took Josie for a walk down the street to the creek. After her meeting with the Indians, the buildings with people in them seemed to offer a modicum of protection.

A half-hour later she returned to find the air around the wagon fresh again so she washed the pot and bowl. She lay down in her wagon bed and thanked God for making the Indians friendly. "Thank You for my new friend, Mr. Noble. Protect me from everyone and everything and help me get along without my parents." She hesitated as a few tears rolled down her cheeks. "Help me not to miss baby William so much. I know he's better off with Rachel and her mama and papa, but I miss him. I love You, God. Good night." She hardly noticed the growling of her stomach and tried not to think about the wasted food. Well, the food wasn't wasted. Maybe Josie's backbone wouldn't stick out quite so far now. Tomorrow would be a better day. She fell asleep listening to mosquitoes buzzing around her head.

৯

Martha wakened early the next morning, feeling the warm sun shining through the white wagon top. She tried hard not to think about the Indians. Thinking how different it would be if her folks were here, she reminded herself that they'd want her to get up and get going.

After carrying back the second bucket of water from the creek (she'd bathed with the first one), she mixed up a batch of trail bread. Josie stood beside her, watching every move she made until movement from the street attracted her attention. She exploded into excited barks.

"Good morning, Miss Lawford," Mr. Noble said. "I have a fresh rabbit for you. Am I too late?"

Martha's stomach made an extra loud growl, and Josie showed intense interest in the dressed animal hanging from the man's hand. "Oh, thank you, Mr. Noble, sir," she said, reaching for it. She wasted no time before washing it, cutting it into pieces, and dropping it into a kettle of water. "This certainly will be a treat," she said. "I thank you more than you know, sir." Josie whined and her sad eyes met Martha's. "Would you mind if I share it with Josie?" Martha asked hesitantly.

"I'd be disappointed if you didn't."

Martha wondered if she should invite Mr. Noble to eat, too, but that would be getting far too familiar at this point. He seemed to be a nice man all right, but she mustn't encourage any man's friendship right now. What did she know about men?

"I'll be back in a while," the man said, interrupting her thoughts. "I'll go see if I can find anyone who needs some washing done. I'll bring back a bar of soap, too."

Martha and Josie each had two pieces of trail bread while they waited for the savory smelling rabbit to finish cooking. "We're going to be so stuffed we won't be able to walk to the creek," she told her dog. But they had no trouble eating the entire rabbit. After they finished, Martha sat on her wooden box, thinking. Not all that long ago she'd have insisted her rabbit be rolled in flour or cornmeal and fried in deep fat with lots of salt. But never had anything, including rabbit, tasted better than this one, boiled in water with nothing else. She had a feeling that Josie, who had eaten two-thirds of the fresh meat, could have had even more.

Well, she might as well try to figure a way to wash clothes. "Come on, Josie," she called, heading east toward the creek. She arrived in five minutes having met not a soul on the walk.

She walked down to the water and squatted. Maybe she could dig a hole in the shallow water by removing rocks. Grabbing stones by the handful, she tossed them downstream. Soon, she had a deep enough spot to dip from or to soak clothes in. She'd roiled the water, but it would soon settle back down.

She looked around. Not a single twig or branch with which to make a fire. If there had ever been any, someone had beaten her to them. She couldn't use her buffalo chips. They were almost gone, too, and she'd never get any more of them. Sitting on the rocks on the creek bank, Martha enjoyed the warm sun on her back. She looked around again. At least she could dry the clothes on the small bushes scattered along the bank. Maybe she could soak the clothes overnight with lots of soap, then wash them in cold water.

"Come, Josie," she called, gathering up her skirt. Maybe she could beat the dog back to the wagon if she really raced. She took off.

Laughing over her shoulder at her surprised dog, Martha nearly ran into a girl about her own age. The girl's frightened shout stopped Martha within touching distance. Martha stepped back a few feet and gazed into the girl's blazing blue eyes. Much shorter then Martha, she looked nice enough, but her round face expressed indignation at being nearly run down directly in front of the boarding-house—her own home. The girl wore a coarse gown of an indescribable color, maybe light brownish gray, and a matching sunbonnet. Her eyes looked as though they'd burst into flame any minute. She looked up and down the street then back at Martha.

"What were you running from?" she finally demanded.

Martha laughed. "Nothing. I just felt like racing with my dog."

The girl stared at Martha, as though trying to figure her out. "Who are you? Where are you staying?"

Remembering her manners, Martha extended her hand to the girl. "I'm Martha Lawford, and I'm really not staying anywhere yet. My aunt and uncle will be coming on the next wagon train. I guess I'll just stay in my wagon until they get here." As she explained she pointed west to her wagon, its dirty white top contrasting boldly against the deep blue sky and the nearly dried grass in the foreground.

The girl's mouth turned into a round *O*. "You're the one Mr. Noble was telling us about. Well, I'm Nellie Martin. Mama and us girls do the boarders' washing. Ain't many other people 'round."

Martha's mouth went dry. "What about the people who run the stores?" she asked. "Do they all live here?"

Nellie nodded her red head. "Most of our boarders own or work at the trading post. We do their washing. A lot of the others live in the back of their stores. They ain't married, and I don't know how they git their washin' done."

At that news Martha felt life flow through her body again. She'd have plenty of people to wash for—if she could just get the clothes clean. "How long have you been here?" she asked. "Do you like it?"

Nellie gazed off toward the Blue Mountains, her fingers curving as she mentally counted. "About eight months," she finally said. "That's when settlers were first allowed in. Mama wanted to own the first boardinghouse. We all worked in a boardinghouse in The Dalles after Papa got his leg smashed off cutting logs. Mama said she could do better than Mrs. Adamson, so we came."

Martha needed to get started washing clothes, but it had been several days since she'd seen another girl. She hoped Nellie would become her friend.

"Come in and meet Mama and my sisters," Nellie said.

"She'd tan my hide if I didn't bring you in. There's only one other woman in the village that I know about."

"Oh, you look so young," Mrs. Martin said. "I hear you've been left all alone in the world. Can I do anything for you, my dear?"

"Would you have work I could do? I know how to clean and I can cook simple food."

A sad look crossed the woman's face. "I'd like to, but we barely get enough money from the men to buy food. One of these days things will be different. But if you don't have anything to eat, you just come eat with us. We eat breakfast at six o'clock, dinner at twelve sharp, and supper at six o'clock in the evening. You just come any time, hon." ·

Martha didn't refuse but she knew she'd have to be *really* hungry to take advantage of the woman's kind offer. Besides, what about Josie? She couldn't eat somewhere and forget her best friend. She almost smiled thinking what Mrs. Martin would say if she asked for food for her dog.

After a few more minutes, Martha managed to get away and ran back to the wagon where Josie waited in the shade. The sun stood almost overhead and Martha felt hungry, but she couldn't think of food until evening. She'd just gather up her tubs and carry them down to the creek. Maybe someone would see what she was doing and offer her some work. If not, she could wash her own things. As she hurried around, Josie announced the arrival of Mr. Noble.

He carried a bunch of clothes, a long-sleeved shirt on the outside with the sleeves and tails tied together to form a bundle. "I found some work for you," he said. Then he pulled a large yellow bar from his back pocket. "Soap, too." His grin looked completely satisfied. "I see you're getting ready. Come on. I'll help you carry the things over to the creek."

"Oh, I can do that, Mr. Noble. It won't matter if I make several trips. I have nothing else to do, anyway." She hopped up into the wagon. "I think I have some paper in here," she called. "I'll just write down the price of the soap." A moment later she jumped lightly to the ground, a piece of dirty, torn paper and a stub of a pencil in her hand. She looked expectantly at Mr. Noble. He grinned. "Well, how much is the soap?" she asked.

"Fifty cents. Is that too much?"

She laughed. "Whatever you paid is the price, Mr. Noble. I won't complain." She wrote **Expenses** at the top and under that she added: *Soap—$.50.*

"Now I feel like a businesswoman," she said, shoving the paper and pencil under the edge of the wagon canopy. Picking up two nested tubs, she started off. Mr. Noble grabbed the clothes and the large bucket, and followed her. "Don't worry about the money, Mr. Noble," she said as they hurried down the street. "I'll pay you as soon as I can."

"Forget the money," he said. "I thought you agreed to wash my clothes in exchange for the soap."

When they both had dropped their burdens on the clean stones beside the creek, they sat with their backs to the sun. "How you going to heat the water?" he asked.

She shook her head. "I couldn't find anything to make a fire. Think I could soak them overnight in lots of soap and wash them tomorrow in cold water?"

A smile tugged at the left side of his mouth before he shrugged. "I've never washed clothes. You wash them and I'll take them back."

Deciding she might as well get the clothes soaking, she rubbed the bar of soap vigorously, trying to make some suds. A few bubbles floated to the top so she continued rubbing until her arms gave out. Puffing, she sat down in the warm sun to rest.

Mr. Noble reached for the soap bar. "Here, let me help with that," he said with a smile. "I'll bet I can work up some suds." Before Martha could object, he grabbed the bar and worked it over. He looked at her, puffing and laughing. "How's that? Think it's ready for the clothes?"

She untied the shirt sleeves and started lifting the clothes into the water. Whew! The stink made her glad they were outdoors. And glad she'd forgotten to bring her own things. She dropped in two pairs of heavy overalls, so filthy they felt stiff, one of which someone had obviously wiped his hand on after blowing his nose onto the ground. She'd never put her clothes into the same water with this filth! She wasn't sure she could put her hands into it. Then she shoved in two unwieldy and equally filthy shirts, followed by a pair of badly stained and malodorous long johns. After she had all the clothes shoved into the water, she pushed them around and around, up and down. She hadn't thought about how seldom these men's clothes got washed. Or what a miserable job it would be. How would she ever get the clothes clean again? Or her hands? If she could find a stout stick she could use that to shove the things around. But there wasn't one stick of any kind anywhere.

Mr. Noble struggled to his feet. "I'll go on back," he said. "I guess you'll leave these things here tonight?"

She nodded, holding her filthy hands away from her body. "They'll be safe, won't they?"

He laughed out loud. "If anyone started taking those

grimy clothes, he'd think again. I've never seen anything safer than that stuff." He gave her a salute and headed west toward the boardinghouse.

She sat enjoying the warm sun for a while, then shoved the clothes around again. The cold water seemed to be doing something. At least it looked almost black. Maybe she should dump it and get clean water. "Thank You, God for helping me get the clothes to wash. I'm sorry I acted like a baby, but I'm purely thankful for having clothes to wash. I love You, Father." Before she added the "amen," she heard a man shouting and cursing. Then Josie appeared, sliding down the creek bank with something bloody in her mouth.

Slick, the man who'd attacked Martha that first day, appeared a moment later with a thick stick in his hand. "Get that dog," he yelled. "It stole my meat and I'm killin' it." Josie splashed across the creek and tore off through the grass, the man following at a much slower pace. About the time Slick stepped from the water onto the other side, his boots dripping, Josie dashed back across to Martha where she then stopped to shake off her excess water. Martha snatched the bloody meat from Josie's mouth. "No!" she said. "Bad dog!" She pointed down the street to the wagon. "Go home, Josie," she commanded. "Go!" The dog took off, looking much less exuberant than she had with the meat in her mouth. Martha wanted nothing more than to give it back to her skinny dog, but she had to make peace somehow.

She met Slick as he stepped from the water. "Here's your meat," she said. "Not even hurt."

He looked at her in surprise, then slapped the meat from her hand to the ground. "You! I shoulda knowed you'd be back causin' more trouble. Well, I ain't eatin' after no dog. Pay for the meat or I'll kill the dog. Take yer pick, girlie."

Martha knew she was dealing with a dangerous man. And for all she knew he might be quoting the law of the land out here in the wild country. "I'll wash your clothes free, Mr. . . .uh. . .I'll do more than enough to pay for your meat."

"Whadda I want my clothes washed fer? Ain't no wimmin out here no how. Just gimme the money and I'll go back to the meat shop."

Not having any money and not knowing what to say, she bent over the tub of dirty clothes and stirred them around.

"Ya ain't got no money, have ya?" he yelled at her. "I know ya ain't." He looked around. "Where'd that dog go, anyway? I'm goin' after the thievin' mutt right now." He bumbled unsteadily off down the street, as if he might have been at the saloon before the meat market.

four

Abe Noble cleaned himself up a little, then decided to go see what was happening at the saloon. Stepping through the front door of the boardinghouse to the dusty street, he heard a rough voice yelling. Sounded like Slick. Remembering Miss Lawford at the creek, he sprinted in that direction. As he neared, Slick lurched off across the street toward Galbraith's Saloon. Abe slowed to a fast walk and continued to the creek.

Miss Lawford leaned over her tub with her back to him. "What's wrong with Slick?" Abe called.

When the girl turned around, she brushed a tear off her face, then quickly faced the tub again, jerking the clothes around.

He stepped down beside her. "Slick been bothering you again?" he asked, fearing to hear the answer. She remained silent. "What did Slick do?" he asked louder than necessary.

He heard a tiny sniff. She jammed the clothes up and down. Then, "Nothing, yet. He's going to kill Josie."

Then he noticed the meat lying on the ground. "Where'd this come from?" he asked, turning it over with the toe of his boot.

Miss Lawford kept stirring the clothes in the black water. She hiccuped loudly, then drew in a deep breath. "Josie took it from Mr. . . .uh. . .Slick."

"Why didn't you give it back?"

Another hiccup. "He. . .he. . .doesn't like eating after

32

a dog."

Abe began laughing. He couldn't help it. Easing himself down to the warm rocks, his back to the sun, he laughed some more.

Finally, Miss Lawford turned to face him. "It isn't funny, sir. My dog didn't mean to do anything wrong. She's been hungry for so long she'd eat anything she could get."

Abe made a determined effort to calm his hilarity. When he had himself under control, he moved to her side. "I know. It just struck my funny bone to think of that old coot eating after a dog." He chuckled again, then managed to stop. "Josie should be the one who wouldn't eat after him, wouldn't you think?" he asked, still grinning.

"I don't know, sir. But I can't let him hurt Josie."

He nodded. "Right. I'll go have me a little talk with Slick. He won't hurt your dog, Miss Lawford. Don't you worry." He almost flinched, watching her soft hands reaching into that grimy water. "Want me to help you get fresh water before I go talk to Slick?" he asked. "I'll make more suds for you, too."

She shook her head. "I can do it, Mr. Noble. Please go tell that man he can't hurt Josie. Please?"

"But I hate to see you working so hard." He took her other tub, filled it with water, then spun the soap bar between his hands until he worked up some suds. He smiled at the appreciation showing in her bright blue eyes. "I'd offer to transfer those dirty clothes but I know you wouldn't let me. So I'm off to talk to the town drunk." He walked a little way before a thought struck him. "Be sure to take that meat home for Josie," he called. Then he strode off to Chapman and Shaffer's Meat Market.

"Seen Slick lately?" he asked.

"Yeah," Will Shaffer growled, "he stoled one of my best roasts about an hour ago."

Abe burst into laughter again. He couldn't remember when his life had been so riotous. "I could return that roast if you want it," he said. He pointed toward the creek. "It's lying out there on the creek bank, quite a lot worse for wear." Then he told the man how Slick had lost the roast and threatened Miss Lawford's dog.

"You just tell the young woman to let her dog have it," Shaffer said. "How was that rabbit you bought this morning? Tough?"

Abe shook his head. "Just fine, Will. Never ate better in my life. You got another one?"

"I got a couple. Want one?"

"Yeah, I'll take 'em both." Abe took the rabbits, wrapped in rough brown paper, and headed toward Galbraith's Saloon. Stepping inside, he waved to a couple of men, then, not seeing Slick, crossed the street to Ball and Stone. He hadn't been in that saloon before but it seemed a likely place to find the man he sought. Slick sat at the bar not far from the door. Abe slid onto the stool beside the smaller man.

"What'll it be?" the barkeep asked.

"How about a bacon sandwich?" Abe asked.

"Comin' up."

Abe turned to Slick. "Heard you lost a little meat this afternoon."

"Yeah! I'm gonna git that dog. Show that high falutin' dame, too."

Abe shoved one of the rabbits down the bar to Slick. "You aren't going to do one thing to that dog, Slick. Remember what happened the other day when you bothered Miss Lawford? Well, that'll seem like a Sunday school picnic compared to what I'll do to you if you so much as touch either her or her dog. Don't push me, Slick. Sometimes I go off like a loaded gun."

Taking his newly arrived bacon sandwich, he hopped off the stool, grabbed the remaining rabbit, and headed for the door. "I hear the city's takin' stiffer measures against thieves, Slick. Better watch it."

"Haw!" Slick snorted. "The way I hear it the town's brand new police force, Sheriff Jackson, ain't even got a gun. Who's doin' all this stiffer measure stuff?"

Abe stepped out of the saloon and drew a deep breath of fresh air. Looking east and not seeing Miss Lawford, he turned west. He dropped the brown paper from the rabbit, making a mental note to pick it up on his way back. Miss Lawford would never accept the rabbit if it came in brown paper. That would smack of charity. Maybe he'd get the rabbit there in time to save her precious trail bread. That stuff didn't look too good, but it must be edible.

As he neared the covered wagon, a small spiral of smoke cut into the blue sky. Then the dog burst from beneath the wagon and came after him as if he were the devil in disguise. Miss Lawford called Josie back.

"Good evening," Abe called when he could be heard. Then he held out the rabbit. "I got lucky again," he said. "This may be the last one in the county though." He hadn't lied, he told himself proudly. He had gotten lucky and it might be the last one for all he knew.

She accepted the rabbit graciously with profuse thanks. "You surely didn't need to dress it out for me, Mr. Noble. That's one thing I learned on the Trail."

When she turned those blue eyes on him, he felt himself melting like bacon grease in the hot sun. He didn't mention it to Miss Lawford, but he'd have shaved that rabbit, hair by hair, and cut it into bite-sized pieces if he thought it would please her.

She washed the rabbit, cut it up, and dropped it into a

kettle of water as she had this morning. "Won't you sit down, Mr. Noble?" she invited after he stood for a few minutes.

After they rested a moment she turned worried eyes to him. "Is that awful man going to hurt Josie?"

He shook his head. "I guarantee he won't hurt you or your dog, Miss Lawford. I just wish I could be sure about every other man in the county."

They visited a while, she telling him about the Indians' visit.

"You mean they just walked off without eating?" he asked.

She giggled. "That's what they did. At first they didn't like it but they soon decided they'd rather have no food than trail bread. They won't bother me again, do you think?"

Abe didn't feel all that sure about the Indians. He didn't know much about them, except they stank and walked into people's houses, expecting to be fed. Everyone he'd known had fed them. He shook his head. "I don't know."

She smiled. "I think they've had more than enough of me. Oh yes, I met Nellie Martin, too." She went on to tell how she almost ran over the girl in her race with Josie. "I hope she'll be my friend. Being all alone, I purely need a friend."

"I'm sure she needs one, too," he said. Then he told how Slick appropriated the meat Josie took from him. "You gave it back to her, didn't you?" he asked.

She nodded. "I did because she's so terribly thin. I hope it won't encourage her to do something like that again."

"It won't." Abe couldn't help noticing how thin Miss Lawford appeared to be, too. Her worn blue dress hung loosely, even at the waist. Then he remembered something. "I checked into the donation claims today."

Miss Lawford sprang from her box. Then she sat down again, but with excitement in her eyes and voice. "How many acres can you get? Can a woman get a claim, too? Tell me about it, Mr. Noble. I purely want one of those donation claims."

"Well, the news isn't all good. The claim for a single person is one hundred sixty acres, for a married couple, three hundred twenty. Yes, a woman can make a claim but a ma. . .anyone must be twenty-one unless they're married to someone who is."

Miss Lawford looked crushed for a moment, then relaxed. "I'll just have to stay with my uncle until I'm old enough," she said with resignation. "But you just wait, Mr. Noble. I'm having a farm of my own."

Abe smiled. "I believe you Miss Lawford. I just wish you could get started right away." *But what if they're all taken before you turn twenty-one?* he thought. Four years is a long time. Wisely, he said nothing to discourage her.

⍦

When Abe finally got into bed that night, Miss Lawford's bright eyes, sensitive mouth, dark hair, and thin body kept watching him while he tried to fall asleep.

"Lord," he said aloud. "You watch over that little girl, hear? I worry about her out there alone." He grinned. "But then You care a whole lot more for her than I do, don't You? I guess I can trust You to watch over her. I'll watch over her all I can, too, God."

He'd never in his life seen such a lovely unspoiled girl. What he'd give to have her on the next farm beside his. What he'd give to have her on his own farm! He finally fell asleep but Miss Lawford invaded even his dreams.

five

Martha shared the rabbit with Josie, even after the dog had eaten Slick's entire roast. Due to Mr. Noble's lengthy visit, the rabbit had cooked so long it nearly fell off the bones. Martha didn't care, neither did Josie. In fact the dog chewed the softened bones and swallowed them.

After supper Martha and Josie sprinted down the dusty street to the creek where Martha gave the dirty clothes a hundred pushes, shoves, and stirs. The water looked as black as it had before Mr. Noble had changed it but she felt far too tired to get clean water again. Walking back to the wagon, she decided to get up early in the morning so she could finish the clothes and they could start drying.

Was this to be her life from now on? She hadn't realized how distasteful the work would be, but who was she, who needed the work so desperately, to complain? What would she do when the weather cooled? Well, she'd just thank the Lord for letting her do it until Aunt Mandy and Uncle Cleve came. They'd never think of letting her do such awful work after they got here anyway. *Bless them, Lord, as they travel. Keep them safe and hurry their steps. Bless Jackson, too, and William.* Her breath came evenly and she made little sleeping sounds before she managed to tack an *Amen* onto the end.

᷍

The sun shining on the worn canopy of Martha's wagon warmed her and awakened her early. "Thank You, Father," Martha prayed out loud, "for the beautiful warm day. Thank You for keeping us safe through the night, too. I love You, Father. I purely love You more than my lips can say." Josie lay on her rug on the floor of the wagon beside Martha's featherbed, which also lay on the floor. When Josie's long tongue gave her an early morning kiss, she bounded from the bed.

"Come on, Josie," she said. "Time to get moving. We have lots to do this morning. Should we go finish the clothes and let them be drying while we eat breakfast?" Josie wagged her plumy tail and Martha took that for a definite yes. She used the last of the water to wash up, then dressed in clean clothes. Maybe if she didn't get more washing she'd do her own this morning, too. Her things would be simple after what she'd been through trying to clean those filthy things in her tubs.

"Come on, Josie," Martha called, taking off down the middle of the dusty street. "I'll beat you to the creek!" Although Martha had a headstart, Josie easily beat her.

Sliding down the short bank to the creek, Martha thought it looked strange. Clean and empty. Then she knew. The clothes, tubs, pail, and everything were gone! "Where can they be?" she asked Josie in shock. "They were here last night, weren't they?" She looked up and down the creek bank. This was the spot. Wasn't it? Then she noticed the hole she'd dug to dip from. And the yellow bar of soap. This was the place all right.

Somebody had stolen her things! Including someone else's clothes! What kind of trouble was she in now? She didn't have any tubs anymore! Nor her big bucket! She sank to the clean round stones. After huddling there for a half-hour, too stunned to cry, she scrambled to her feet and turned her face heavenward. "What did I do to deserve this, Lord?" she cried out loud. "I thought You promised to be with us always. Where were You? And what am I supposed to do now?" Her strength gone, she dropped to the smooth stones again, but this time she curled into a small ball. Josie sat down, leaned against Martha, and proceeded to wash her upturned ear.

After a while, Martha reached around the big dog and pulled her close. "Oh, Josie, what would I do without you?" she asked, rubbing her pet behind the ears. As she fondled the dog, her internal tumult quieted, and she began to put this last blow into perspective. Yes, it was bad. She needed those tubs and bucket. And she had no idea what would happen when the men learned their clothes were gone. But this was nothing compared to what she'd already been through. She'd suffered the most severe blow a young person could sustain—losing Mama and Papa. And Petey, the little boy she'd cared for all the way from Independence. *Why? Why, Lord? If You'll just tell me what I'm doing wrong, I'll quit.* As she lay quietly thinking, Josie suddenly jumped away and began barking, her fur bristling.

"I thought I'd find you here," Mr. Noble said, sliding down and dropping to a sitting position beside her. "What's going on? You didn't sleep down here, did you?"

Martha popped into a sitting position. "No, but you can see we should have. Sit down, Josie. He won't bother us."

Mr. Noble looked wide-eyed at Martha, then glanced around. Finally, he nodded as if understanding her pain. "What happened to your things?"

She shrugged. He didn't respond. "The coyotes got them?" she asked with a tremulous smile.

His sympathetic chuckle rewarded her bravado. "How long have you been here?" he asked.

"We got here about sunrise."

He sat quietly a moment, then stood up. "We know who did it, of course."

"We do?"

"I threatened to hurt Slick bad if he bothered you or your dog. He thinks he can get away with this, but he can't." He stood quietly a moment. "Come on, you may as well go back to your wagon." They walked back together. When they reached the wagon, Mr. Noble showed Martha a dressed duck he'd shoved onto the wagon floor. "You go ahead and do whatever you planned. I'll see you later," he added, hurrying away.

"Thanks for the duck," she mumbled so softly he might not have heard. Do whatever she'd planned? If she didn't feel so awful, she'd laugh at that. Well, at least she didn't have to touch those filthy clothes anymore. She probably should be thankful for that. Maybe those men would never figure out who lost their clothes. That was another laugh. Didn't she just have lots to laugh about today?

She cut up the duck then remembered she needed water. In ten minutes she returned with the small drinking bucket filled to the brim. She washed the pieces of meat, put them in the kettle with a little water, and sat down to do some more thinking.

"Hello, there," a cheery voice called. "I came to visit." Martha looked up to find Nellie Martin almost beside her. Suddenly, she felt lighter.

"Hi," she returned, pointing to the two wooden boxes. "Sit down, Nellie. I'm glad to see you." Then she noticed something in Nellie's hands.

Martha's new friend handed her a piece of chocolate cake on a small, chipped, blue-bordered plate, then sat down. "Mama thought you might like this. Thought you might not have a way to bake." She took in the fire with the kettle over it. "Guess she was right."

"Thank her for me, Nellie. We'll really enjoy the cake."

"We?"

Oops. "I'll enjoy it, Nellie. I'm used to saying 'we' to my dog."

Nellie looked around some more. "Want to take a walk? Oh, I guess you're fixing something to eat. I'd better go." She stood up.

Martha stood up, too, but feeling lightheaded, sat back down. "I guess we'd better eat now, but could we take a walk afterwards?"

Nellie thought she could and after promising to come back later, left.

"Well, Josie," Martha said, "let's dig in. Thanks to Mr. Noble our flour is holding out pretty well." Martha had heard you shouldn't give dogs fowl bones as they're sharp and brittle, but she had no idea how she'd keep them from Josie. The dog ate half the duck and all the bones. Then they divided the cake. Martha got impatient when Josie swallowed her half of the cake without chewing it even once. "I may as well have eaten it all," she grumbled. "You didn't even taste it."

☙

About midafternoon, Nellie came back so the girls walked north to the creek. "Mill Creek carries a lot more water in the winter," Nellie said as they tossed small stones into the tiny stream. "Let's take off our shoes and wade."

Mill Creek. So that's what it is, Martha thought.

They both took off their shoes and stockings, held their skirts up, and waded up and down the creek, slipping on the slick rocks. Josie ran in and out of the water, exploring the dried grass, weeds, and all the delicious smells on both sides of the small stream.

"It feels nice and cool," Nellie said just before her feet went out from under her. "It's cold," she screamed, laughing, making no effort to regain her feet. ·

The girls spent an hour playing in the water, Martha being careful not to fall. How would she ever wash her clothes now? She wanted to tell Nellie about her latest calamity, but for some reason kept it to herself.

After they finished, they sat in the sun, drying, for another hour. The sun felt so good and a delicious smell, almost like ripe berries, wafted around the girls.

"What are those buildings on the other side of the creek?" Martha asked as they rested.

"Oh, you mean on past the street? That's old Fort Walla Walla where the soldiers lived during the Indian wars. In '57 they moved a couple of miles west of the street. The soldiers are still there to put down any Indian uprising. They're just not as close as they used to be."

"I see. What's going to happen to the buildings?"

Nellie shook her red head. "I don't know. Maybe someone will take them in a donation land claim." Jumping to her feet she tried to brush the wrinkles from her dress. "The sun's getting low. I'd better get back to help with supper. You can't even tell I've been wet, can you?" she asked, spinning around merrily.

Martha raised her eyebrows. "I'll bet your mother can tell," she said with an impish grin. "Will you be in big trouble?"

Nellie cocked her head, then shrugged. "She never looks at me so she won't know. But she'll notice if I don't get back to help with supper."

They hurried back, Nellie to the boardinghouse, and Martha to her covered wagon. As Martha watched her new friend disappear into the boardinghouse, she marveled at how much she'd enjoyed the day in spite of her ever increasing troubles. Maybe she'd see Nellie a lot. A good friend would make life much more bearable, even if it wouldn't bring back the missing clothes and tubs.

The sun leaned far into the west and Martha's stomach told her it was time to eat. She fixed a batch of trail bread, making a little extra as they hadn't been using it all the time lately. As she and Josie ate, she wondered if Mr. Noble had found Slick. Hopefully he had, and the missing clothes and utensils as well.

Martha's walk to Mill Creek with Nellie that afternoon had honed her curiosity, so she decided to walk south now. She'd seen some buildings in that direction and felt that she might as well investigate. Walking some distance, she discovered a few shacks widely spaced. Maybe these people had taken donation claims but she feared to venture too close. She'd ask Mr. Noble about the crude buildings the next time she saw him.

She didn't have to wait as long as she'd expected because as she neared her wagon his long frame unfolded from one of the boxes by the fire pit. "Hello," he called. "I began to think you'd grown disillusioned with our little town and left."

She laughed. "And how would I go about doing that?" She watched him a moment as he sat back down, apparently with nothing in particular to say. "Did you find my things?" she asked.

His lips stiffened into a straight line as he shook his head. "Slick's not in town today. First time since I been here."

She almost felt glad. "Well! That proves he did it."

"Not for sure. But he did it all right. Those clothes

weren't worth stealing. And no one else has it in for you."

Martha leaned forward on her box. "What about the clothes, Mr. Noble? Will they throw me in jail?"

His dark eyes sparkled. "This town don't have a jail. Wouldn't put you in one if they did." Still grinning, he shook his head. "I don't know what'll happen when they find out. The local sheriff don't have any deputies or help." He chuckled. "It's rumored he don't even have a gun. I guess it's up to the fellers who lost the clothes. You got nothing they could take and no money to pay so I guess you're all right." He stood up. "I'd better be gettin' back to my room." He stretched and looked at the western sky. "About to get dark, too." He took a few steps away from the wagon and turned back. "You just get a good sleep and don't worry none," he said. "I'll probably see you tomorrow."

Martha watched him, almost silhouetted by now, until he disappeared, not through the door, but around the boardinghouse. "Wonder what he goes around there for?" she asked Josie. Receiving one thrash of the dog's tail for an answer, she continued. "Think he's getting tired of us?" she asked. "He seemed pretty quiet this evening." She hugged the big soft head to herself. "We can't blame him. We're causing him a lot of trouble."

Something caused Josie to give a little start. Martha released her. "All right, it's not us that's causing the trouble. It's just me. C'mon, let's go to bed."

⁊⁊

Martha lay in bed, swatting at mosquitoes, when she heard men's voices. Josie bristled and a growl formed deep in her throat. Martha held the dog tight, whispering "Shhhhh" in her ear as the men stood outside the wagon, talking.

"Think she's in there?" one voice asked.

"Shore. Where else could she be?"

"Let's wake her up. She's the purtiest thing in town."

The other man snorted loudly. "Ain't a lot a wimmin to choose from, Len. But we ain't wakin' nobody up. Next time we'll just git ourselves here earlier and let the lady decide for herself which of us she likes."

Martha hardly dared breathe until the footsteps died away. Even then she feared to slap at the buzzing insects. *Please, Lord,* she pleaded silently into the darkness, *protect me until Aunt Mandy and Uncle Cleve get here. I'm getting purely scared.* She lay stiffly, controlling her breathing, for over an hour. Finally, she fell asleep holding Josie close.

six

As Abram Noble poured oats into Charity's manger box, he thought about Miss Lawford. How could she stay so sweet and calm in the face of her problems? When he was alone, her delicate face laughed into his thoughts more often than he cared to admit. Never had he seen such bright color and depth in anyone's eyes, such utterly rich dark hair, and thin straight body. She looked young. Several years younger than her age. But that might be to her advantage right now. Few men would bother a young girl.

Charity's soft nicker interrupted his thoughts. "You want more?" he asked. "You realize I haven't ridden you once in the last week? You aren't burning up much oats that way." He forked a couple of scoops of hay into the manger. The mare nibbled contentedly while Abe closed the gate and went to his room.

❧

The next morning, after breakfast, he headed to the Ball and Stone Saloon. After ordering a cup of coffee, he asked about Slick.

"Ain't seen him fer a couple o' days," the bartender said. "That's the way I like it."

Abe nodded. "Yep. Me, too, but I gotta see him. Know where he hangs out?"

The man didn't, so Abe left. He crossed the street and went into Galbraith's. Not seeing Slick, he ordered another cup of coffee. "Seen Slick around?" he asked, sipping the strong hot brew.

The man wiped the shiny board-top of the bar and shook his head. "Not for a couple o' days. Hope he's left the country."

Abe chuckled. "Well, I do and I don't. I gotta see him first. After that he don't have anything I want." He finished his coffee and headed off toward Miss Lawford's wagon. He stopped, turned around, and then headed back to the meat market. If those kinfolk didn't hurry up, that girl would be destitute. He'd help where he could. He surely did believe she'd starve before she'd take charity. Let her dog starve, too? Now that seemed a different matter. She thought more of that dog than most men did their wives.

"Why don't you just keep the paper?" he asked Chapman when the man started to wrap the rabbit.

The rustic-appearing man laughed out loud. "Abe, I took you for a man who wanted to keep things kinda clean. Losin' my knack of judgin' people, I guess." He carefully laid the paper aside for later use.

Abe couldn't help telling the man his problem with Miss Lawford. "So you see if I brought it all wrapped up, she'd refuse it right off. I don't rightly know what'll happen to that girl if her kinfolk don't get here before the snow flies."

The man winked at Abe. "You'll just have to take care of her, Abe. Now ain't that an awful pass to come to?"

Less then five minutes later, Abe walked into Miss Lawford's camp. "Did you find him?" she asked right off.

He shook his head. "Not yet, but I will. He can't get along without his booze forever." He held out the rabbit. "Guess I'm too late for your breakfast."

"Yes, but I'll put it in some water and we'll have it for supper." She flashed him a radiant smile. "I can't thank you enough, Mr. Noble. Your extra meat helps us so much." She looked into his eyes. "It *is* extra, isn't it?"

He assured her he'd had all he could eat for breakfast.

She nodded. "Good. Oh, yes, Mr. Noble. I have something I've been wanting to ask you." She pointed south and east of them. "Do you know what's going on out there? I saw some buildings. Think they could be people getting donation claims?"

He nodded thoughtfully. He needed to get busy and find the perfect spot for his claim. Why had he been dillydallying, anyway? He didn't know what, but something seemed to keep him from moving ahead with his longed-for plans. Well, yes, he did too know what. He kept trying to figure a way to get Miss Lawford on the claim next to his. It looked impossible though. She lacked a lot of years of being old enough.

Miss Lawford's voice brought Abe to the present. "Is there any way I could find out about the shacks?"

"We could go ask them."

Her face colored. "Oh, I didn't mean that. I'd be afraid to bother anyone."

He got up. "I'm not. I'll go get Charity and we'll have ourselves a little ride. She's been needing some exercise, anyway. Might be interesting." He hurried away, forgetting to say goodbye.

≈

The mare nickered when Abe entered the barn as if glad to see him. "Well, you're goin' to get to see a little of the country around here," he told her as he threw the saddle over her back and cinched it up. "Think you're up to a heavy load for a while?" he asked, gently inserting the bit

between her teeth. Charity nuzzled his neck as he took
the reins and led her out the door. Outside, he swung into
the saddle as if he were used to it. And he was. He and
Charity had ridden lots of miles together when he'd been
in the army. He patted the shiny neck as they turned
toward the wagon.

He wouldn't mind at all sitting close to Miss Lawford
for a little while. He patted Charity again. "I'll be careful
not to overload you though," he whispered softly.

Then Miss Lawford and Josie ran to meet them. "He
has a horse, Josie, a beautiful horse," he heard her say as
they ran.

"Whoa," Abe said softly, taking the slack from the reins.
When Charity stopped, he slid off. "Ready, Miss Lawford?
I'll help you aboard."

Martha looked at the trim horse. "What about you, sir?"
she asked.

"I'm riding, too. I wouldn't do it if you weren't so tiny,
even though everyone else treats their horses that way. A
horse shouldn't carry more than ten percent of its own
weight. I've seen three people pile onto a horse, then
force it to gallop. I've seen horses with bad swaybacks,
too. I've even seen people force horses to run until they
died." He stopped with a jerk. "Well, I didn't mean to
get going on that," he said, puffing. "We'll just take good
care of Charity here."

Miss Lawford moved back a few feet. "I can walk,"
she said. "Josie and I'll just walk along beside you."

"No. Charity won't mind for a little while. We won't
run her and we won't go very far."

"Sure?"

"Sure. Get over here." He settled her behind the saddle,
then easily swung himself up, doubling his leg as it cleared

the saddle, so it didn't bump Miss Lawford. He handled the reins gently and Charity turned south. "You just put your arms around me," he said. "I got stirrups to hold me and you don't."

"We could have all walked. It isn't far at all." Miss Lawford reached her thin arms around him but Abe could barely feel her. She must be reluctant to be so close. And to touch him.

He nodded. "You just hang on tight, Miss Lawford. You could crack a bone if you fell off. I know we could have walked and enjoyed it." He grinned and wiped his forehead. "I don't know why but a horse gives a man a little authority." He leaned forward and stroked the sleek neck. "You'll be all right, won't you, girl?" He looked east and pointed. "You mean those buildings there?"

"Yes. And a few more."

Turning the mare eastward, they walked straight to one of the ramshackle buildings, Josie running and frolicking alongside. "Whoa," Abe said softly, pulling his leg awkwardly back so he wouldn't kick Miss Lawford as he slid off then helped her down. She took hold of Josie's collar.

A man, who'd been digging with a shovel, looked up. "I c'n do somethin' for you folks?" he asked.

"Yes, sir," Abe answered. "We're interested in a donation claim and wondered if that's what you have here."

The man pushed the shovel into the ground with his foot and let it stand. "Shore is." He spun around looking at the vast expanse of dried grass and tall weeds. "Ain't it a beaut though? Got me three hundred twenty acres. A year from now I'll be harvesting wheat or somethin'."

"I guess I'll have to be satisfied with one hundred sixty acres," Abe said. "But that's a lot, too."

The man glanced at Abe, then Martha, and shook his

head. "You can get the same as me and my woman if you hurry. Who knows what they'll do next year."

Abe and the man talked a few minutes discussing the steps involved in taking a donation claim, then Abe said they should be getting back.

When they reached some distance from the man's place, Abe turned the horse toward another shack south and off to the west. Charity walked sedately to the shanty and Abe climbed off. Miss Lawford slid off before he could help her, called Josie, and held her collar. A woman opened the door with a child on each side, hanging onto her skirt. "You'uns want somethin'?" she asked in a trembly voice that sounded fearful.

"We just stopped to say hello," Abe answered, hoping he sounded harmless. "I'm hoping to get a donation claim, and we're just talking to people, finding out what we can."

The woman nodded, pushing back the strands of grayish hair that had fallen loose. "That's what we got here. Rube isn't here. He could tell you about it better 'n I can."

"That's all right. How can you tell where your property ends?"

The woman finally smiled. "It goes on a long ways. Three hundred twenty acres we got ourselves here."

Abe cast a glance at Miss Lawford. "Thanks for taking the time to talk to us. Maybe we'll be neighbors one of these days."

After another short ride they stopped at a raggedy tent and dismounted.

"Looks pretty quiet," Miss Lawford murmured. "I wonder if anyone's around." She took Josie's collar. For the first time the dog pulled against her and growled. Martha's hand tightened on the collar.

Just then a matted gray head poked through the canvas

doorway. "Whatcha want?" he asked.

Abe almost choked when he recognized Slick's thin voice. "We came to see you, Slick. Better come out."

After a long wait the filthy man pushed the canvas door aside and stepped out. Miss Lawford stepped back ten feet; Abe almost did, too. How the man could stand to be in a small unventilated tent with himself, Abe couldn't imagine.

"Where are the things you took from the creek?" Abe asked.

Slick blinked. "What things you talkin' about?" he asked.

"You know what I'm talking about, Slick." Abe's voice didn't sound so harmless anymore. "You bring them out or I'm coming in after them."

Slick backed up a few feet. "I don't know what you're talking about, boy, but you got the wrong man. I been right here tryin' to git over the flu for almost a week."

Abe shoved the canvas tent door apart with both hands and stepped inside. It took a moment for his eyes to adjust, and the smell turned his stomach. Dirty clothes covered a filthy looking sleeping bag. Several tin dishes lay scattered over the dirt floor. Then he saw the tubs and bucket. Stacked neatly inside each other, they appeared to be the cleanest articles in the smelly tent. Abe grabbed them up and carried them outside. Setting them down, he backed off and took several deep breaths. "How do you stand yourself and that tent?" he asked. "That smell's enough to knock a good man down."

Slick pointed at the tubs and bucket. "What you doin' with them things?"

"We're taking them. They belong to Miss Lawford. Where's the clothes, Slick? She'll be in trouble if she doesn't return the clothes."

Slick snatched at the utensils. "Them's mine and you ain't takin 'em nowhere," he whined.

Abe met Miss Lawford's eyes. "Are they yours?"

She stepped over and looked at each one separately. "Each of my three are different and these're just like mine. Strange he'd have three exactly like mine." She shrugged. "But I don't know."

Abe nodded. "Yep. A little too much coincidence. Look here, Slick, are you ready to stop messing with Miss Lawford? I'm about to send you out of town faster than you came in. No one in this town would cry, neither." He picked up the bucket and stack of tubs and set them down beside Charity. "Come on, Miss Lawford, let's get you up there." A moment later he picked up the things again, swung into the saddle and held the large pieces of equipment to his side. "Come on, Charity, just a little farther."

As the horse moved away, Josie, growling deep in her throat, jumped on two feet toward Slick. Slick screamed. Before Abe could move, Miss Lawford hit the ground and threw herself onto the big dog.

"Josie, stop," she said, grasping the dog's collar. Josie yielded to Martha's touch, calming down. "You go on, Mr. Noble," she called. "I'll have to bring Josie."

Abe wheeled Charity around between Slick and the girl. "All right," he said softly. "You go on. I'll be right behind you." He turned to Slick, whose eyes still bulged half out of his head. "I'm not warning you again," he told the man. "This is it. Next time you cause either of us any trouble you're out of here. Come on, Charity, let's go find some air we can breathe." He turned the already prancing horse and took off at a gallop after Martha.

seven

Early the next morning, Mr. Noble brought Martha another rabbit. "Josie and I can't thank you enough," she said. "Where you getting them, anyway? I watched last night and didn't see a thing."

Mr. Noble smiled. "You think they'd come out with Josie there?"

She nodded as she cut up the meat and put it into the kettle to boil.

"Say," he said, "I found the perfect place for a claim. How'd you like to see it one of these days? It's just a little ways. You can ride Charity and I'll walk with Josie."

"Mr. Noble, why don't we both walk? I'd enjoy it. If you have that much time, that is."

"We'll see. Charity would enjoy having you ride her, though. Do you like to ride?"

Martha nodded enthusiastically. "I love to ride. But not when I make the horse's owner walk."

Mr. Noble hurried back to town. Martha took the rabbit from the water, cooled it, and divided it with Josie. After they finished she let Josie drink the cooled juice the rabbit had been cooked in. The dog licked the kettle so clean that Martha couldn't find a drop on it.

She'd just finished washing the dishes and kettle when two men rode up. The brown-and-white spotted horses they rode hardly compared with Mr. Noble's sleek bay mare.

"You the girl who's washing our clothes?" the dark

whiskery one asked. Neither man dismounted.

Suddenly, Martha felt so lightheaded she had to sit on one of the boxes. Why hadn't she prepared for this meeting? It had to happen. *Help me, Lord. Show me what to say and don't let them get mad at me.* The men didn't really look mean, but everyone around looked tough. Then she noticed their filthy clothes. They owned the clothes all right. Their overalls looked just as filthy as the ones she'd lost. But what could she say? Well, Mama had always taught her the truth was the easiest and best.

She cleared her throat and hung tightly to Josie's collar. "Yes sir, I am."

The dark-haired man nodded. "Any idea when they'll be ready? Folks around here don't have too many clothes."

Her mother's voice spoke plainly into her ear. *Tell the man the truth, Martha!* She nodded. *Yes, Mama. You're right.* "I'm afraid I have real bad news about your clothes, sir."

The younger fellow with the light-colored, shaggy hair gave a short laugh. "What? Them clothes was so dirty they fell apart when you washed them! I figgered that'd happen."

Martha couldn't help giving him a little smile. Then she shook her head. "They didn't fall apart. They totally disappeared." Seeing their surprise, she went on. "I had to wash them at the creek because they were so dirty and took so much water. I washed them twice the day I got them then left them soaking overnight on the creek bank and when I went back the next morning they were gone . . .and I don't know what to do." She took a long deep breath.

The horses moved a little in the silence that followed Martha's outburst. She could see sympathy in the younger man's eyes. Maybe the older one, too.

"I'm sorry to hear that," the older man said. "You got any plans to find the clothes? And what ya gonna do if you can't find 'em?"

Martha found some strength and stood beside the man's horse. "I don't know yet, sir. I don't have any money. That's why I was washing clothes."

The man turned his horse. "We'll be back in a few days to see what you figgered out. When someone goes into business, 'e usually knows what 'e's doin'." He touched his horse's sides and they tore off toward the street.

Martha released Josie's collar. "Well, what's going to happen to us?" she asked the shaggy dog. "I guess they still don't have a jail." She went inside the wagon and looked at the calendar she'd made. She checked off today. *Thanks for being with me, God. I was purely scared. Are you watching over Aunt Mandy and Uncle Cleve, Lord? They should be here by now, and I'm getting into a worse mess all the time. Please bring them soon. I need them, and Jackson, too.* She didn't know if Jackson, her older brother, had met the wagon train her uncle, aunt, and cousin were with. He should have by now. He really should have, and they should be coming down off the Blue Mountains already.

❧

That night, rain splattering on the wagon canopy woke Martha. She snuggled deeper into her covers. Hopefully the top would keep her dry. It had before during a light rain. Then she remembered the times every wagon had to be emptied so everything could be set out to dry. What a mess! She dropped her arm over Josie who slept beside her, and fell back to sleep.

But she awakened again sometime later, cold and wet.

She couldn't do anything in the dark and had no place to go where she'd be out of the rain. She pulled Josie into her bed and put Josie's rug over them. The dog helped warm her some, and the rug helped a little, but before long both dog and girl were thoroughly chilled. As she lay holding the dog close she wondered what she'd do in the morning.

She must have fallen asleep, for she awakened with a start to face daylight. A moment later she noticed she didn't hear rain anymore. "What are we going to do, Josie?" she asked her wet but warm pet. "At least you don't have to put on cold wet clothes. Well, you don't, because you're wearing them."

"Are you in there, Miss Lawford?" Mr. Noble's soft voice called through the soaked cloth wagon top.

Oh, oh. Now she not only had to get into wet clothes but she had to do it in a hurry. "I'm here," she called. "I'll be out in a minute." Josie didn't have anything holding her back so she jumped down, eager to greet her new friend.

Martha could hardly bear to take off her warm wet nightgown and put on her cold wet clothes. Everything stuck to her but she finally got changed. Then she brushed her hair, braided it, and put it up.

Martha jumped to the ground to find it had turned to mud during the downpour. After a quick feeling of defeat she looked up to find Mr. Noble watching her.

"I knew you'd get soaked," he said. "You can't stay out here much longer you know. It's going to rain a few times, then it'll turn to snow." He had a rabbit in his hand but didn't offer it to her. "You're freezing right now, aren't you? Come to the boardinghouse with me before you catch pneumonia."

She couldn't do that! She couldn't get more indebted to this man than she already was. She'd been writing down all the meat he brought and what she thought it would be worth if she'd bought it. But she'd never be able to pay a boardinghouse bill. Never!

"I'll be just fine," she said, trying to smile through chattering teeth. "As soon as I get a fire going I'll get warm." She pointed toward the east. "The sun's going to shine, too. Just you wait and see."

"Let me help you get the fire started then." He jumped into the wagon, returning a moment later with a handful of buffalo chips. After working for some time, the chips caught fire. Wordlessly, he picked the rabbit off the box he'd laid it on and handed it to her.

She washed the rabbit and cut it up, then dumped it into the kettle to cook.

"Do you get tired of eating the same thing all the time?"

She flashed a nice smile. "When I'm not so impoverished I'll worry about getting tired of something. Right now I'm happy to have anything for Josie and me to eat." She sat down on the box, hoping the fire would dry her clothes.

He sat down on the other box. "I hate to bring this up, Miss Lawford, but it seems to me your kin should be here by now. Anytime now the Blue Mountains will be blocked with snow, lots of snow. It might have snowed up there last night."

Martha's heart shrank a little in her chest. She knew even better than he did what a terrible position she was in. She couldn't hold back a strong burst of shivering. "I don't know where they are but they have to come soon. They just have to." She blinked hard. She wouldn't cry. Not in front of Mr. Noble.

He got to his feet. "I'm leaving for a while. I'll be back." He stood quietly, just looking at her for a moment. "You have to face the facts, Miss Lawford. If you insist on staying here in the wagon, I'll come out here some morning and find you with pneumonia or worse. As if you aren't in enough trouble, you're out of chips." He turned and strode toward his boardinghouse.

eight

Abe slammed up to his room, hardly seeing Nellie, and not speaking as he passed her. He tipped up one side of the chiffonier and grabbed his money pouch from under it. Dropping to the bed, he dumped the contents on the smooth quilt. Barely noticing the gold pieces, Miss Lawford's delicate but cold form thrust itself into his mind. He'd never seen anyone so brave—man, woman, or child. Those brilliant blue eyes had sparkled with unshed tears this morning but she'd held them back.

His eyes clouded as he wondered if she were crying now with no one but Josie to see and comfort her. He simply couldn't handle the way things were going for Martha Lawford. Something had to be done. Now!

He sat up and stacked his $100 gold pieces in piles of ten. He hadn't used any of them since he got here so he still had thirty. Then his $50 nuggets. Nine of those. His paper money and coins added up to $337. He pulled out a piece of paper and pencil and added his figures—$3787. And then there was the $490 he kept in the top drawer as a decoy. He gave all the pieces an angry shove, jumbling them together. He had plenty of money to last until he could begin making more. Why couldn't he use some of it to help Miss Lawford? Ever since he'd met the girl he'd thought of almost nothing else. She was everything he'd ever wanted in a woman, so why was she sitting outside in the cold and rain while he had a warm dry room?

"Show me how, Lord," he cried. "I don't want her to

suffer or get sick and die! You don't, either, Lord. I know You don't! Please show me how to help her."

Sadly shoving his money back into the pouch, he once again lifted the chiffonier and laid the bag under so it didn't show. He sat on the edge of the bed, his chin cupped in his hands and his elbows on his knees, deep in thought.

You could marry her, Abe. He could marry her! He could marry her and take care of her! In his elation, he jumped to his feet.

Then he sank back to the bed. What made him think she'd ever have him? She was scared to death of men—the sex to which he had to claim membership. More than once she'd shrunk away from him when he'd accidentally touched her. And she'd never given him the slightest reason to think she felt anything for him, other than gratitude.

"That's not it, Lord. She'd never do it. Even if she wasn't fearful, she's plenty proud. She'd call it charity." He shook his head thinking about it. There had to be another way.

You really could marry her. He shook his head again.

Then a new thought popped up. The I and R building wasn't occupied. Maybe he could rent that for her and fix it up. "Yeah!" he said out loud, finally wearing a wide smile. "Thanks, Lord," he said, not realizing the Lord hadn't said anything about renting a building for her.

But the owner of the building planned to open his own business in it almost immediately.

Abe left, dejected. As he crossed back to his place he decided he might as well check on Miss Lawford to see if he could do anything to help her dry out her wagon and things.

When he turned west, he thought his eyes were playing

tricks on him—three wagons stood where only one had this morning. Probably her kinfolks! He tore off to the wagons at top speed, trying to decide if he really was all that happy they'd come. Would she decide she didn't need him anymore?

Arriving, he found several children playing around the wagons, ten oxen grazing on the nearly dried grass and weeds, and four adults talking to Miss Lawford. Several substantial pieces of wood lay on the ground beside the blazing fire. Every sturdy weed in the area supported some article of clothing or bedding.

"Hello, Mr. Noble," Miss Lawford called. "Come meet my new friends."

He soon learned Miss Lawford hadn't known them until an hour or two ago. "Where you headin'?" he asked after a while.

The men laughed cheerfully. "We ain't heading nowheres," the short one said. "We just found it. Ain't this what they call the land of many waters?"

Abe nodded. "Reckon as how some do. Got several streams running around the place. It's also called Steptoeville or Waiilapptu."

"We're collecting us some donation land claims," Wilford, the tall one said. "Miss Martha tells us we can get three hundred twenty acres each. That's enough for us."

"Did you folks get wet last night?" Abe asked.

The women shook their heads. "We spent the night near the burned out mission. Nary a drop did it rain." She smiled at Miss Lawford and patted her arm. "Sure got Martha, though."

Unkind thoughts skittered around in Abe's mind. These people just arrived this morning. How did they have the right to call Miss Lawford by her Christian name already? Did she invite them to? She sure hadn't told him he could. He forced his mind back to the company. "I see you got your things drying, Miss Lawford," he said. "Sure hope it don't rain again until your kin gets here." He turned to the standing men again. "I guess you folks don't know anything about her kinfolk's wagon train."

They both shook their heads. "No," Wilford said. "We just come from the Willamette Valley. I reckon we'll be finding us some claims and moving onto 'em purty soon. Gonna have to work fast to get cabins built before bad weather comes."

Abe nodded. "Sure are. I'm doing the same thing. Gotta quit messing around and get busy myself." He started away from the wagon. "See you again, Miss Lawford. Glad you're getting dried out."

"Thanks again, Mr. Noble," Miss Lawford said. She giggled softly. "I'd likely be dead if you hadn't helped me so much."

❧

Those people would no doubt be telling Miss Lawford right now to watch out for him, he thought, rushing back to his room. He sat in the rickety rocking chair in the corner of the room, thinking.

He really should go ahead and get his claim settled and build his own cabin.

Marry her, Abe. Abe thoroughly liked the idea. That would solve all their joint problems. She'd be able to get a claim now while they were still available. She wouldn't be out in the cold and rain with nothing to eat. He'd be able to care for her as he longed to do. It hurt him deep inside to see her suffering so. Then with a shock he realized he loved her! He'd loved her almost since they first met.

He looked up and discovered he'd been rocking furiously. Slowing to a sensible pace, he smiled. He loved Martha! What a beautiful name for a beautiful girl, inside and out. A girl with plenty of pluck. He shook his head. He couldn't file his claim without her. He'd talk to her the first time he got her alone.

Then he remembered he'd promised to take her to the spot he'd found for the claim. Maybe he could get her away from the others to go look. He grabbed his hat, tore down the stairs, and ran out the door.

"I just remembered inviting you to go see a purty parcel of land," he said when she came to meet him. They'd stopped a few feet from the others. "Think you could get away for a little while to see it?"

She glanced toward the others and shook her head. "I don't know. What do you think?"

He smiled into her sincere blue eyes. "I dunno," he said. "Are you entertaining them? Or are they just waiting to file their claims?"

She grabbed his arm. "Can we go right now?" He nodded. "I'll be back in a little while," she called to the people around her wagon. "Come on, Josie."

He led her south of the buildings, then east behind them. "It's right on Mill Creek," he said, cutting back southeast.

In a few minutes they stood on the bank of the small stream. Trees lined the creek bank almost until it reached the street. Probably people had cut those in the way of the street. He turned south and held his arms out to his sides, his hands facing the property. His heart thrilled every time he stood in that spot. "Well, what do you think?" he asked.

She looked. She looked up and down the creek, then

her eyes moved over the large expanse of land. "It's the most beautiful piece of land I've ever laid eyes on," she said quietly. "I purely wish I could get a piece right beside you. Oh, how I wish I were twenty-one!"

Abe wanted more than anything in the world to ask her to marry him. And she'd made it so easy. He could tell her she could have her 160 acres right now. He could tell her he'd take care of her forever. He could tell her he loved her! Her deep blue eyes gazed into his, her full lips slightly parted, waiting. But he couldn't get the words past the mountain-sized lump in his throat. He tried several times but nothing came out.

"Come on," he finally croaked. "Let's get you back to your friends."

Leaving her just before they reached the other people, Abe decided he might as well look around some more; at least he'd be giving Charity some exercise.

nine

Martha stood where Mr. Noble had left her and watched him stride down the street. He'd been in a strange mood. First he'd been jolly and talkative, then he hushed right up. She hoped she hadn't offended him in some way. Well, she'd better get back to her new friends.

"Say, is that fellow more than a friend?" Mr. Tynnon asked. He shoved his stringy blond hair back and grinned at Martha.

She shook her head. "Just a friend, but the best friend anyone could have. Why do you ask?"

Mrs. Tynnon stepped over to Martha. "Honey, didn't you see how he looked at you? That man had stars in his eyes."

Martha shrugged. "You misread him, Mrs. Tynnon. He's just a really good man."

"Why did he have to take you off alone then?" Mrs. Nelson asked. "He's sweet on you, young lady, and a mighty fine looking man he is, too. You won't find any better in a small place like this. Maybe not anywhere."

"Mind if we stay the night here with you?" Mr. Tynnon asked. "Tomorrow we can find our claims and get out of your way."

"That would be nice," Mrs. Tynnon added. "We could get—Timothy, drop those clothes!"

Martha looked to see the little boy dragging across the muddy grass most of her clothes as well as her bedding with Josie on the other end. She jumped up and rescued them. Only a little muddy, she put them away before they got worse. Shoving them into the wagon, she decided she could fold them later.

"I'm sorry I can't invite you for supper," she told the visitors. "I have only a wee bit of flour to eat. I mix it with water and call it trail bread but I have only about a quart left."

Mrs. Nelson made a face. "That's all right," she said too quickly. "We'll just share the fire. You go ahead first, child, and when you're through we'll cook our meal."

Embarrassed, Martha mixed some water into half her flour and cooked it in her pot.

"That stuff smells funny," one of the children said as it cooked; his mother told him to hush.

When the bread was ready, Martha divided it with Josie, who gulped it down without complaint. Just as Martha had finished eating, the two men whose clothes she'd lost, rode up.

"Howdy," the older one said, tipping his ragged, filthy hat. "Your kinfolks finally got here, I see."

Martha shook her head. "No, these folks came from Oregon City. My aunt and uncle will be here in a few days."

Mrs. Tynnon smiled again. "In the morning we're going to find ourselves some donation land claims."

"Congratulations, I'm sure." He reined his horse around until he faced Martha again. "What have you figured out, Miss Lawford?"

Martha shook her head. "I didn't find the clothes. . .and I still don't have any money." Suddenly, she remembered her father's clothes in the wagon. Although she felt sentimental about them, she certainly didn't need them. She looked up at the big dark-haired man and smiled. "I have some clothes in the wagon you might be able to use."

Not a flicker of emotion crossed his face as he said, "Get them."

Martha clambered into the wagon, shoved aside the bunch of clothes and bedding she'd just put in, and opened the tattered black trunk. Her throat clogged as she pulled out two pairs of dress pants, three dress shirts, underwear, and five pairs of black dress socks. Hugging the garments to her chest, she realized once again that Papa would never again be with her in this world. *I needed him so much, Lord, she cried silently. When am I going to see some signs of the love I know You have for me?* She swallowed, secured a tighter grip on the clothes, and jumped to the ground.

The young blond man hadn't said a word, just sat quietly on his nervously moving horse. But when she handed the clothes to the older man the younger one burst into loud laughter. "I can just see you in that stuff," he howled through his glee.

The big man said nothing until he'd sorted through each and every garment. When he finished, he shoved the clothes back toward Martha. "Ain't a thing there a man'd wear," he growled. "Looks like preacher clothes."

Martha shook her head. "They're not," she whispered. "Those were my father's clothes. He was a farmer and these were his Sunday clothes. Don't you wear Sunday clothes sometimes?"

"Not like that stuff!" the younger man said, still laughing.

The older man glared at her for a moment, then his face softened. "I see you got the tubs back." She nodded. "The clothes weren't in them no more?"

Martha swallowed hard. "We found the tubs in a man's

tent but the clothes weren't there. We'd have taken them if we'd found them."

"Know the man's name?"

She nodded again, then wondered if she should tell. Why not? She couldn't think of any reason to protect Slick. No reason at all. "He's called Slick. That's all I know. I think Mr. Noble knows his name, though. He lives at Martin's Boardinghouse." She pointed south. "Slick's living in a tent out that way."

The man wheeled his horse away from the group. "Thanks," he grunted as the horse burst into a gallop. The younger man touched his horse's sides and took off after his friend, or father, or whatever he was. Martha shuddered as they headed south.

Martha carried the clothes back into the wagon and repacked them in the trunk. She could tell that her friends wanted to know what the men wanted but she said nothing.

Noticing the women preparing food, she climbed back into her wagon and put away her clothes and bedding. She fervently hoped she'd not endure another rainy night like she had last night while she still lived in the wagon. She jumped to the ground and saw a kettle on the fire, boiling briskly and starting to fill the area with a tantalizing fragrance. She asked what they were cooking.

"It's just a soup," Mrs. Tynnon said. "We put in some wild onions we gathered near The Dalles, some potatoes we brought from Oregon City, and dried meat and salt. Nothing special."

A little while later they called the four children and began serving up the soup, the most delicious food Martha had ever smelled in her entire life. When she decided they weren't going to offer her any, and Josie began running from one to another, begging, she called the dog and took off down the street. Just smelling the food wasn't very satisfying for either of them. She put her arm around her faithful friend's neck as they walked. "I'm sorry, Josie, but those people didn't want us to have any. You just wait. One of these days you'll have all you want."

She turned right, walked past the empty building on the end of the street, and followed the creek as it turned east to the spot where she and Mr. Noble had stood earlier today. Yes! This was exactly where she'd want her farm. Exactly here. She'd put her house right over there on that little mound where it would be high and the grass would never grow brown. She looked in every direction, trying to imagine how far 160 acres would go. A long, long way.

Facing the creek, the only thing she didn't like was the sight to her left of the old abandoned Fort Walla Walla buildings. What would happen to those buildings, anyway?

She sighed and turned back to face the land Abe had shown her. How could the Garden of Eden have been more beautiful? She'd love to have this piece of ground. But it would surely be taken before she turned twenty-one. Then she laughed out loud. This place already belonged to Mr. Noble. He'd shown it to her in the first place. She cast her eyes eastward. The next place would be just as good. She'd be perfectly satisfied with it. She'd enjoy being Mr. Noble's neighbor, too. But all the good places would be taken within four years.

"You like it?"

Martha jerked around to find Mr. Noble standing behind her, looking over her shoulder at the land spreading before them. She nodded. "I even figured where to put my house before I remembered this is your piece of Washington Territory."

He swallowed and looked at her as if he were in pain . . .just as he had this afternoon. He didn't reply.

"Are you all right, sir?"

He still didn't answer but stood looking across the expanse of grass, weeds, and the few trees along the stream, his Adam's apple jiggling spasmodically. Finally, he met her eyes and smiled. "Show me where you'd build your cabin."

She laughed, a happy tinkling sound. "I said I'd build a house, sir, not a cabin." She laughed again, joyously, and ran to the small rolling knoll she'd thought to build on. "Right here," she called, standing in the middle. "Don't you think this is a good place?"

He nodded but said nothing.

"You don't like it, do you?" she asked, realizing she felt unreasonably disappointed. What difference did it make to her where he built his house. . .cabin?

After hesitating, he nodded again. "I do like it, Miss Lawford, but I thought I'd build a couple hundred feet farther up the creek." He beckoned with his hand and she followed him, feeling nice and warm in the autumn sun and realizing the luxury of the feeling.

He finally stopped on another small rise. "How's this?" he asked, his soft brown eyes boring into hers.

She nodded. "Fine, except there aren't any trees."

"I'll plant some," he said, his eyes starting to get their usual sparkle again. "Fruit trees, shade trees, and whatever else you. . .I mean *I* want."

Martha couldn't be sure but she thought Mr. Noble's tanned face turned rosy. "I don't know much about trees," she said, "but I like these that our Lord planted. They look just right."

He nodded. "I think they're locust trees. I could probably find some small ones and bring them over here and replant them. I'd have to do it a little later when they're sleeping."

"That sounds good. Well, Josie and I'd better be getting back to the wagon." She met his soft brown eyes again. "I'm not sure why but I like it alone better than with those folks."

"They leaving soon?"

"Tomorrow they say."

"All right. I'll probably see you then." He hesitated a moment then turned to follow her. "I might as well see you get back to the wagon safe."

Neither talked as they walked behind the buildings, Josie running circles around them. Martha's thoughts kept going back to one pint of flour and no buffalo chips at all. And those people knew it and didn't offer her anything at all. But they had a lot of people to feed and maybe they didn't have much food either. Maybe.

Mr. Noble stopped before they reached the wagons. "I'll go back now," he said. "I hope you'll enjoy your guests tonight."

"Thanks," she said. "Goodbye." She turned, dreading to have to spend the evening with the Nelsons and Tynnons. Maybe she'd go to bed early. Last night had been bad and she hadn't gotten much sleep.

"Well," Mrs. Nelson said with apparent glee, "look who brought you home."

"What did he do, take you out for an ice cream?" Mr. Tynnon asked.

Martha laughed. "I'm afraid you won't find any ice cream in Steptoeville. This is just a little western settlement. Maybe some day you'll find fancy things, but not yet." She stretched. "I hope you won't mind if I go to bed early. I didn't get much sleep last night and I'm tired. Come on, Josie."

The next morning Martha built a fire with the newcomers' wood and made the last of her flour into trail bread, trying to forget the lovely smells from last night. As always, she shared her meager meal with Josie, who swallowed the small bit and begged for Martha's half. Martha chucked it down as quickly as she could. "I'd give it to you, Josie," she whispered, "but I'm already weak from not eating."

The occupants from the other wagons still slept so Martha and Josie walked to the creek again, following it south then east for some distance. The bright sun on her shoulders made her feel good even though she literally didn't know from where her next meal would come.

They walked farther east than she and Mr. Noble had last night and she found trees bordering the creek again. Trying to see everything, she decided this land was even prettier than Mr. Noble's.

After she felt completely alone, she knelt by the bubbling stream.

"Thank You for the warm sunshine, Lord," she said out loud. Josie came and sat beside her, licking her closest cheek. "Two days ago I didn't appreciate it but now I realize what a precious blessing it is. Six months ago I didn't even appreciate good food, but I do now. Oh, I really do now. Lord, You know how it is with me and I know You have something planned so Josie and I won't starve, but we're both hungry now. We'll try our best to be patient if that's what You want, and if we're doing something to displease You, show us, Lord, so we can stop. I love You, God, and purely want to please You. Thank You for Your past care, and Your future care, too. We pray in Jesus' name. Amen."

She sat on the bank of the creek, her arms wrapped around her knees, enjoying the busy sound of the stream rushing over the rocks, the bird calls from the meadow floor, and the warm sun on her back.

Somehow her mind went back to the long, long trip over the Oregon Trail. She thought of the times when they traveled several days without water, without either water or feed for the stock. And the times the oxen dropped in their harnesses and died on the spot. And the crossings of the Snake River. They'd thought that some of the other streams were hard, but they didn't know hard until they crossed the mighty Snake.

They'd lost a yoke of oxen when it had been swept down the wild stream, and one wagon had been turned over and destroyed. But worst of all was that a little five-year-old boy had drowned. A little boy she'd played with and helped care for during the entire trip.

Just before that, Mama had sickened, and then Papa had come down with it the day before Mama had died. He'd never known she died. In fact, he'd thought Martha had been Mama the last day of his life.

Martha bowed her head into the circle of her arms as they lay on her knees. *It's been hard, Lord. And it's still bad. What should I do? Even out here in nowhere land there has to be a way to get food for Josie and me. I'm willing to work hard. Just show me, Lord, and I'll do it. Anything.*

She sat quietly until Josie nuzzled her arm and made a sound half between a bark and a growl. Martha lifted her head and laughed. "You're telling me to get up and get going, aren't you, Josie? Well, let's go." She scrambled to her feet, giving the big dog several pats in passing, then pulled up her skirts and took off running back toward town. She'd stop at every business and ask for work.

She found rough men in every building. The two whose clothes she'd lost seemed to own the tin shop. They, as well as all the rest acted like gentlemen, and expressed sorrow over having to decline her application for work. Most of them ran their own businesses and barely made a living without hiring anyone.

The barkeeps told her they'd be afraid to hire her for her own safety, that there weren't half a dozen women in town. When she left the last building, feeling depressed, she noticed her wagon stood alone.

"Josie," she said, taking off running, "they're gone." She stopped running and stood looking at her wagon. "I didn't think I'd ever be happy to be alone, but I am." She hurried to the wagon. Then she remembered she had nothing to eat and no way to make a fire even if Mr. Noble brought her something. "At least we'll be alone so we can starve in peace, won't we, Josie?" she asked, still feeling lighthearted for some strange reason. She had no food, she'd just learned there was no work for her in Steptoeville, and she felt happy? She remembered reading in the Bible how the birds didn't work, nor the lilies of the field, but God took care of them. Then it went on to say how much more valuable people are than birds or flowers. That meant her. God loved her more than the birds or lilies.

She sat down on one of the dynamite boxes to rest, feeling she'd had a busy morning although she'd done nothing but learn there was no work for her. . .and remember the awful trip west. She fell deep into her thoughts again and didn't hear the horses until they almost reached her.

"Whoa, Charity," Mr. Noble's soft voice murmured. "You got no call to be skittish with Sampson." He stepped down from the saddle and led the two horses up to the wagon.

Martha met him. "You have another horse, Mr. Noble. It's beautiful just like Charity."

Mr. Noble smiled. "Nah, he ain't like Charity. She's a lady through and through. He's just an old nag I picked up."

ten

In his excitement, Abe's legs barely held him up. In the few days he'd been looking, he'd been lucky to find another horse of Charity's quality. Darker than Charity and with a creamy mane, tail, and socks, the horse made a pretty sight. Martha had to like him. He stood two hands taller than Charity and, though spirited, he'd be easy for her to ride.

"Come ride with me," he said, holding his breath for fear she'd refuse. He'd made up his mind that today he'd ask her to marry him. No matter what, he'd do it this time.

She shook her head. "I don't know if I should," she said. "Besides, you don't have a sidesaddle."

"A sidesaddle? Come on, Miss Lawford. No one out here uses a sidesaddle. Don't you know they're dangerous? That dress you have on is plenty full to be perfectly modest."

Miss Lawford's clear blue eyes looked questioning as though it might not be proper.

"I have something important to do," he said, hoping to tempt her. "Somebody beat Slick Collier almost to death. I found him in front of the saloon this morning and hauled him out to Fort Walla Walla. I need to see if he's still alive."

Miss Lawford's eyes opened wide, her face paled, then her hand flew to her mouth.

"Why do you act like that?" he asked.

She opened her mouth to speak then shook her head. "I better come with you," she said. "Will you teach me to ride straddle?"

Abe laughed. "You'll know how right off, and wonder how you ever stayed on that sidesaddle. After one ride you'll never sit one of them crazy things again."

"Let's get me on then. Is the horse friendly?"

"Yeah, he's great." He met her eyes for just a second. "Don't think I'd let you ride him if he wasn't, do you? Here, put your left foot in the stirrup and I'll boost you as you swing up." She did as he instructed and sat in the saddle as if she'd been riding straddle forever.

Sampson danced a little but quieted when she gently firmed the reins and talked to him. "I feel as if I'm on top of the world," she said to Abe. "He's awfully big."

Feeling secure in the way she handled the big chestnut, Abe mounted Charity. "How you doing? Want to take it easy for a while?" he called over his shoulder to Miss Lawford.

"Oh, Mr. Noble, I love him. I purely love him. We're doing fine and we're ready to do whatever you do."

Abe touched Charity's sides with his knees. "Come on, girl, let's hurry," he said softly. The sleek horse stretched her front feet forward into a long lope that covered the ground in a hurry. Behind him, Miss Lawford called Josie to come along. The less than two miles would have been a nice run for the horses, but after a half-mile Abe reigned Charity in and Miss Lawford and Sampson slowed   beside him.

"I love Sampson," she said, "and I love the speed, but I'm glad we slowed because Josie's not strong enough right now to run very far."

In a few minutes the dog caught up and trotted beside

Miss Lawford and Sampson, her tongue hanging out the side of her mouth. No need to mention that Josie was the reason Abe had slowed to a walk.

"How far out is Fort Walla Walla?" Miss Lawford asked.

"We're almost there," Abe replied.

"Do you have any idea what happened to Slick?" she asked.

He shook his head. "Someone beat him to a bloody mess. Beyond that, not a hunch. Do you know something?" She didn't answer but he had a gut feeling she did. Why didn't she tell him?

As they rode quietly along, he stole quick peeks at her. Just the curve of her chin and neck left him breathless, as did the long dark lashes over her bright eyes. "You ride like you been riding straddle forever," he said. "How d'you like it?"

"You're right. It's the way to ride." She looked behind them. "Come on, Josie, just a little farther."

Abe saw the Fort Walla Walla buildings and pointed. "There's the fort. We're here already."

In a few minutes someone invited them into one of the log buildings and called a doctor to talk to them. They waited on a rough bench in a big room with tables, probably the eating hall. Several braided rugs covered most of the unfinished wooden floor.

Finally, a very tall man dressed in buckskins and having long brown hair that curled on the ends, a full beard, and a thick mustache approached. "You related to Slick Collier?"

"No, I'm the one who found him and brought him out here. Didn't know what else to do with him. How is he?"

The doctor shook his head. "I didn't find any broken

bones, but he's barely breathing. I guess we'll just have to let him rest and see what happens." He stopped and drew a couple of breaths. "Learn anything about what happened?"

Abe shook his head then glanced at Martha. . .Miss Lawford. Why did he keep using her Christian name in his mind? Pretty soon he'd do it to her face and that might mess things up. And why didn't she tell the man what she knew?

She said nothing.

"How long before you have an idea whether he'll make it?" Abe asked.

The doctor shrugged. "Dunno. Maybe tomorrow, maybe a week."

Abe got to his feet and shook hands with the doctor again. "We'll probably be back tomorrow."

⁂

As Martha and Abe took their time returning to the wagon, Josie, who had recovered some, trotted beside the horses. "Think Josie'd stay at the wagon if we went for a longer ride?" Abe asked when they neared Steptoeville.

She shook her head. "Not unless we tied her or something. She thinks she's my guard."

When they reached Miss Lawford's wagon, Abe looped the horses' reins over the tongue of the wagon. "I got a couple of things to ask you about," he said. "You got time to talk?"

She laughed. "No, I'm sorry, sir, but I have a formal ball to attend tonight. Would you like to make an appointment for next week?"

He grinned back at her, turned the boxes upright, and shoved one toward her. "Sassy little thing, ain't you? Well, I need to hear what you know about Slick's accident."

She sighed, hesitated a moment, then answered. "I thought you'd ask me before the day ended." She wound her hands around each other then released them. "I don't know for sure, but I have an idea." She told him about the men whose clothes Slick had stolen, and about her telling them who'd taken them and where he lived. "It looks like they beat him, don't you think?"

"No!" Abe said, louder than he meant to. "Those boys are tough but they'd never hurt anyone." But even as he denied it, he came to feel she was right. "Well, what do we do about it?" he asked.

"I don't know what happened," Miss Lawford said. "Why don't you talk to the men?"

Abe thought a moment, then shook his head. After all, he'd given Slick a licking, too. Slick seemed to provoke a man to do that. First and foremost in his mind was what he wanted to ask Miss Lawford. He grinned. "Maybe I'll just let it alone. Slick kind of affects people that way. If a chap has only two sets of clothes it might not set all that well to have someone steal one of them."

She nodded, looking as though she were a million miles away. He got up. "Reckon we could go for a walk?" he asked.

"Sure. Where?"

"I don't care."

She hopped from her box and took off south; after passing the buildings, she veered east.

Abe followed and Josie trailed after him. A few minutes later, they reached Mill Creek. She followed it south until it turned east and then followed it some more.

Finally, she stopped. "This is where I want my claim," she announced. "Right beside yours."

Abe felt his heart give an extra thump, then sat down

on some clean rocks. He patted the rocks beside him. "Come, sit down. I need to talk to you."

She complied, then looked into his eyes. "Sounds serious."

He shook his head. "It's a serious subject, but that doesn't mean bad. In fact, it's good. The nicest thing I've thought about for a long time. No, it's the nicest thing I've thought about. . .ever." He stopped for breath hoping she'd say something to help him but she didn't.

"I've kinda grown used to you in the last little while," he started out. He stopped. That sounded like getting used to new shoes. Maybe shoes that hurt his feet at first. He'd better tell her how he felt about her or she'd never accept him.

He cleared his throat and started over again. "I mean, Miss Lawford, that I. . .do I have to keep calling you Miss Lawford forever? What's wrong with Martha and Abe?"

She giggled and tossed a small rock. "Martha and Abe are good. I like them just fine." The rock disappeared into a deep pool, sending out ripples to both banks.

Hope spread through his chest like the ripples from the stone. Maybe this wouldn't be so hard after all. He'd just spit out the plain words and see how she took them. He cleared his throat again. What if she said no? What if she hated the thought of it? What if she hated him?

Well, he'd never know until he asked. He pulled in an extra deep breath and rubbed a shiny circle on a round, whitish stone. "I've been thinking about you a lot lately," he finally managed. "I've been wondering. . .I've been . . .what are you planning to eat now that your food is gone and your buffalo chips, too?" As soon as the words left his mouth he hated himself for them. That could completely cloud the issue. He wasn't asking her to marry him because she was going to starve. He loved her and wanted to care for her the rest of their lives.

Her ivory complexion lightened almost to white, and she shook her head slowly. Picking up a head of dry grass, she tossed it into the water. After a time that seemed forever, her brilliant eyes met his. After a serious moment, she smiled and a twinkle crept back into her eyes. "I guess I'm going out somewhere and starve to death. Josie will go with me. She's hungrier and skinnier and weaker than I am." She reached both hands behind her and leaned on them, thinking. "Truly what am I going to do? I don't know. My uncle and aunt are way, way overdue. Maybe they'll come this afternoon."

Abe wanted to lay his large brown hand over her small white one, on the smooth rock. But he resisted the temptation. "You can't spend your life watching down the Trail for your kinfolks." He wiped the sweat from his forehead, knowing the day wasn't that warm. This was the time for him to ask her, but he didn't want her to think his proposal came from sympathy. *Good going, Noble. You just demolished the most important moment of your life.* He raised his eyes to find her looking at him with a question mark in hers.

"Martha," he spluttered. Then he rushed on before he had a chance to think up any more stupid ideas. "I want to marry you," he gushed so quickly she probably couldn't even understand his words.

eleven

Martha couldn't believe her ears. It had sounded as though Abe wanted to marry her! She watched a large brown bird, probably an eagle, circling in the clear blue sky above them. Abram Noble would never ask her to marry him! Never! Yes, she'd misunderstood his garbled words. She met his eyes. "I'm sorry," she said softly. "I'm afraid I didn't hear your last words."

Mr. Noble sighed then hesitated, as though unable to repeat it. Terror shot through Martha's veins like boiling water. He had! She'd heard him right the first time. He'd asked her to marry him!

"Uh, I asked you to marry me," he mumbled again. He jerked in a quick breath and went on. "I love you, Miss . . .I love you, Martha. I've loved you since I first laid eyes on you. Marry me and we'll build a house right here on the creek."

For some reason, she had to struggle for each breath. She'd never known a nicer man in her life, and she purely liked Abram Noble a whole lot. But she'd read lots of books. When she fell in love, she expected to see fireworks, hear bells ring, trumpets blare, flutes trill; then she'd feel a pink cloud wrap tightly around her. But right now she heard only a donkey braying down the street, and saw a puff of dust blowing across the creek.

Finally, she lifted her eyes to discover his kindly brown ones staring at her, apprehension etched in his entire face. How could she hurt him? He'd been so good to her. "I'm so shocked I don't know what to say," she whispered. "I had no idea. I had no idea at all. Could I have a little while to think about it?"

A small degree of relief relaxed his face. "Sure. You think as long as you want." He struggled to his feet and gave her a hand up. Neither said a word as they strolled back to her wagon; both hearts were too full.

As they reached their destination, he turned to leave. "See you later," he said in a muted voice as he walked off.

Martha dropped heavily to one of the dynamite boxes. Josie crowded against Martha, leaning her big head in Martha's lap. "What do you think of that?" Martha asked the big dog. She waited a moment then went on. "There never was a nicer man. But I have to be in love before I marry, so don't go getting excited about it." She sat staring off into the blue, wondering how she could tell him without hurting him, her hands idly caressing Josie's rough fur.

Then an entire new line of thought came to her. If she married Mr. Noble she wouldn't have a thing to worry about anymore. She'd have plenty to eat, a nice home. Josie would have enough to eat, too, the first time in a long time. She'd probably have a horse of her own . . .Sampson. As she thought about it she realized that Mr. Noble had no doubt bought Sampson mostly for her. Oh, what a nice man!

But she didn't love him! She'd read books about girls that married men for their money. She'd never do that to any man but especially not to Mr. . . .Abe. He was too fine a man to treat that way. *Oh, Lord,* she cried silently, *help me tell him without hurting him. I know you wouldn't want me to marry him for convenience, and I don't want to. But Lord, I'm in about as bad a position as a girl can get into. You know of course, but I'll tell You anyway. I don't have any food or fire to cook it with if I had it. Won't You help me get something to eat? Thank You, in Jesus' Name. Amen.*

After praying, she felt really hungry. Before, she'd been able to put it from her mind somehow, but now her stomach rumbled and she felt ravenous. Almost instantly she thought of the gun in the wagon. She didn't know how to shoot it but maybe she could learn. But, if she managed to kill something, how would she cook it? Her eyes fell on the myriad of large weeds surrounding her. Maybe they'd burn! She laughed. They'd probably burn like paper and be gone almost instantly.

Well, she might as well give it a try. Dragging the gun from the wagon, she sat down on a box and examined it. She had to put a shell in it but had no idea where. After looking at it for a while, she put it back in the wagon. She'd never figure it out alone. Maybe she could go ahead and gather up some of the weeds and see how they burned.

Show me what to do, Lord. Thank You for caring for Josie and me. Before she said "Amen," she saw a figure coming toward the wagon. Nellie Martin! And she held something in her hand. "Thank You, Lord," she said aloud. "I know You've answered my need as soon as I asked." She hurried to meet Nellie. "Hello," she called. "You don't know how glad I am to see you."

Nellie took a couple of skips and held out a brown package. "Mama made a loaf of bread for you," she said. "It's still warm, and she even sent some butter. I hope you're hungry."

"Oh, Nellie, you just don't know." When Martha took the bread, the smell made her so hungry she plopped down on a box, feeling weak. She'd been wishing Nellie would come see her again, but suddenly she desperately wanted her friend to leave so she could eat. She felt so hungry her legs actually shook. Then her eyes fell on Josie and her heart fell. The dog could eat the whole loaf in two gulps and still be hungry.

Nellie's voice brought Martha back. "I have to go back now, but I'll come see you tomorrow if that's all right."

Martha nodded, clutching the aromatic package in her hands. "Yes, come back, Nellie. We can take another walk."

Nellie barely turned away when Abe arrived, a rabbit in his hands. "I got a rabbit for Josie," he said, laying it in front of the skinny dog, who snatched it into her teeth and ran under the wagon with it. "Sorry I didn't find any firewood. I will though by tomorrow." He left immediately, too.

Finally, at long last, Martha pulled the golden loaf of bread from the brown paper. A loaf of real bread! It looked as good as it smelled. She'd had her last real bread the first few days after they had left Independence six months ago.

"Thank You, Lord," she said out loud. "I've never been more thankful than I am now, and You provided for both Josie and me almost before I asked. Thank You again. Amen." She tore the end off the bread and took a big bite without waiting to spread the butter. It tasted like manna from God. And it was.

Sinking onto the box, she concentrated on eating slowly. If she didn't, she'd eat the whole loaf without a thought for tomorrow, just like Josie. When she finished the first piece, she forced herself to put butter on the next one, and the next. When she'd eaten almost half the loaf, she wrapped it back up in the brown paper, even though she wanted more in the worst way. Would she ever again have all the food she wanted?

Josie chose that time to come out from under the wagon, licking her lips. The dog hadn't saved any for tomorrow, Martha noticed. When her pet started sniffing toward the brown paper, Martha took it into the wagon and put it inside the trunk. That bread would at least be a few bites for them tomorrow.

⁖

Later, when she lay on her featherbed, she thought about Abe's kind offer of marriage. It would be so nice to have someone to care for her, to know she'd have plenty of food every day, and a warm dry place to sleep. It wasn't as if Mr. Noble. . .Abe were mean or unkind. He wasn't. He'd even thought of Josie tonight when Martha couldn't cook.

Wait! He brought food for Josie at almost the time Mrs. Martin sent Nellie with food for her. Could that have been coincidence? Hardly! Mr. Noble had arranged it all. Yes, no doubt about it. She looked skyward and folded her hands. "Lord, is Abe my raven? I know You're sending me food through him as You did Elijah through the ravens. Thank You, God. And thank You for Abe. I've never met a nicer person, Lord. Do You think I should go ahead and marry him?" She almost felt she should.

Then she remembered. They could get 320 acres! Twice as much as either could get alone. Besides that, the land would probably all be claimed before she turned twenty-one. Yes, she'd better forget her silly romantic ideas and get on with life the best way she knew. But she couldn't do it. That would be the meanest trick in the world to play on Abe.

❧

Early the next morning, she awakened to find frost on the ground. She took her morning sponge bath in cold water. Brrrr. It had been so much nicer when she could heat the water. She pulled on a clean brown dress that looked as if she'd walked across the country in it. She giggled because that's exactly what she'd done.

"Shall we divide the bread now or wait?" she asked Josie. The plumy tail wagged several times.

Before Martha could decide, Abe brought another loaf of bread, warm from the oven as the last one had been. Josie sniffed and grew restless.

Abe sat on one of the dynamite boxes and looked at her in a strange way. "Will you marry me, my little Martha? I'll be so good to you and care for you and love you with all my heart."

She couldn't do it. She owed him too much to hurt him by pretending something she didn't feel. Through almost unbearable pain, she shook her head. "I'm sorry, Mr. Noble. . .Abe. Josie, get back from this bread. I owe my very life to you and, more than words can say, I appreciate what you've done. But I would only hurt you if I married you, because although I consider you the best friend I've ever had, and purely know you're the kindest man I've ever met and I respect you more than anyone I've ever known, I don't love you as a woman should love a man she marries."

He flinched as if she'd given him a hard right to the chin and then he sort of wilted into a crumpled heap. He didn't say a word nor did he move. He just sat there, leaning forward, his elbows on his knees.

Seeing the pain in his eyes, Martha leaned over and put her hand on his arm. "I'm so sorry," she said. "I almost said yes, but I realized I'd be marrying you for the wrong reasons and that I'd hurt you more if I married you than if I didn't." She pushed back Josie's inquisitive face from the warm bread she still held. "You're a true friend, Abe, and it's hard for friends to hurt each other."

He shuddered and stood to his feet, smiling down at her. "It's all right. I had no reason to believe you cared for me. I—"

"Oh, but I do care for you, Mr. . . .Abe. I care for you very, very much, as a dear friend."

He smiled again, a tight smile that came out almost a grimace. "It's all right, Miss Lawford, don't give it another thought. I'll probably see you tomorrow." That was it. He rushed down the street without a backward look, his shoulders hunched.

Somehow, Martha no longer felt hungry for the bread she held in her lap. Josie had been trying to get her attention ever since Mr. . . .Abe had given her the bread. "Come on, Josie," Martha said wearily, "I'll get you the rest of yesterday's loaf." She patted the faithful head and climbed into the wagon to exchange the new loaf for the old. When she climbed down, she held out the bread. "You need it more than I do," she said.

She sat back on the dynamite box, watching Josie eat the bread in three quick bites, chewing each only a few times. "Well, our problems are still alive and healthy," she told the dog. "We still don't know where our next meal is coming from. . .and it's getting colder every night."

twelve

As Abe walked back to his boardinghouse, he decided he knew how a bullet in his heart would feel. He'd never known such pain in his life. Could he live without Martha? Would he actually die from the pain as he would a bullet?

He rushed straight to his room, avoiding talking to or even meeting anyone. Easing down to his bed, he closed his eyes. "I tried, God," he prayed aloud. "Is this the way You want it? How long will I hurt. . .forever? I don't think I can handle this that long." He rested a few moments while a single tear ran from his right eye, across his cheek, past his ear, and onto the coarse muslin sheet. "She'd starve if I didn't take her food. I'm not sure I can stand the pain of seeing her. But You know I can't let her get too hungry." He lay quietly thinking for a while. And the pain continued. "Could You just take away the pain, God? I'd be thanking You a long time if You'd just do that for me." But the pain continued.

He fell asleep. When he awakened, his mouth tasted awful and he felt blacker than his shaded room. How could he live in the same world with Martha and not be able to call her his own? He pushed open the faded denim curtains to find the sun had moved into the western sky. Abe had the distinct feeling God had been talking to him while he slept. He sat up and thought hard, unable to remember.

Dropping his feet to the floor, he tried to think but couldn't get past his pain. He grabbed his hat and jacket and went out to check on the horses. Even though the sun still shone most of the time on these early November days, it didn't have enough strength to warm the air much.

When Charity saw him coming, she nickered and trotted to the fence. Sampson followed, almost reluctantly. "You're my best girl, aren't you?" Abe said to the horse, rubbing her neck and shoulders. Sampson shoved his big head against Abe's hand. "Oh, you want some, too, eh?" Abe said, pleased to know the big horse was beginning to care.

Abe gave both horses some oats and headed for the saloon.

"Heard about Slick?" the barkeep asked when Abe settled onto the stool.

Abe shook his head, reaching for the coffee he'd been served. He'd forgotten all about Slick. The man might be dead—small loss.

"Well, he got beat up the other night," the barkeep announced. "Someone hauled him out to Fort Walla Walla, more dead than alive. But I hear he's about well now. Purty hard to get rid of a skunk like that."

So, the old geezer lived. Abe couldn't tell whether he felt relief or disappointment. His own intense pain crowded out all other emotions.

Abe ate a roast meat sandwich without tasting it, then wondered what Martha had eaten that day. Sure would be a lot easier to feed her if the poor dog wasn't always twice as hungry. After ordering another sandwich wrapped, he hurried to the meat shop where he ordered a rabbit. Upon being told the rabbit was for a dog, the butcher offered him a bunch of meat scraps at no charge, adding that he could pick up scraps every day.

Abe, carrying the sandwich in one hand and the big bag

of scraps in the other, headed for Martha and Josie. He straightened his shoulders. He'd act as if he'd forgotten all about the proposal and rejection. He'd just be a casual friend again. *But how could he do that?* He just would, that's all there was to it. He would.

She walked to meet him, a worried look on her face. But why should she feel bad? She's the one who'd said no. He forced a big smile to his lips. "I just learned you can get free meat scraps for Josie every day at the meat shop," he said in a superficially cheerful voice. He handed her the sandwich and dumped the scraps onto the grassy ground for Josie, who snatched up a meaty bone and retreated to her special spot under the wagon.

"Come sit down for a while," she invited.

He complied. "Have you been noticing how cold it's getting at night? Not too warm in the daytime, either."

She nodded. "I know I can't live in the wagon all winter. Thankfully my uncle and aunt are coming. I've been having a feeling it will be real soon."

He nodded. "It better be." He pointed east at the bluish, snow-capped mountains. "Have you noticed we get new snow in the Blues about once a week now? They may be impassable already and it's going to get worse in a hurry."

"I know. They'll be here soon," she said with a weak giggle. "I just have a feeling in my bones it'll be soon." She swallowed. "I guess I'm not very grown-up, not being able to care for myself and all," she added in a tight murmur.

"It's hard for a woman," he said. "How can a woman earn money here? The only possibility I see would be working in one of the saloons, and you let me know you weren't interested in that."

She hung her head, her face pink. "But I did try," she whispered as if confessing to something indecent. "I tried both of them and they said no." She sniffed. "I tried all the businesses. No one wanted me."

He felt another stab. This time for her pain. She'd tried her best, done everything she could, and still she sat here helpless and hopeless. He draped another smile across his face. "Good thing your kinfolks are coming soon," he said, getting up. "I better be getting back. Mrs. Martin wants her guests to be on time for supper. Guess I don't blame her much." He took a few steps and turned back. "You eat that sandwich yourself, see? Josie still has some meat scraps." He smiled a genuine smile. "How long has it been since she walked off and left food?"

Martha laughed softly and shook her head. "I can't even remember. Thanks, Abe, you're the best friend I ever had. Josie, too."

*

He hurried to his room where he washed up, then rushed on to the dining room.

"You ain't looking so good," Nellie said when she sat down across the table from him.

"I'm all right, Nellie, just hungry." He didn't feel hungry at all but had already made up his mind to eat all he could force down to keep up his strength.

When he finished eating, he went out to see the horses again. "I should take each of you out for a ride," he told them, "but I don't seem to have the hankering right now." He lumbered back to his room and flopped down onto his bed. Martha didn't look any happier than he felt. Well, she had plenty of problems, even if a broken heart wasn't among them. How would it feel to be a girl in this country with nothing, not even food, and unable to find work?

It would be awful, no doubt, but would it hurt as bad as what was hurting him? Finally, he shook his head. Probably as bad but different.

Abe, I want you to marry her.

"I tried, God," he cried out loud. "You heard me. What are You talking about?"

Your broken heart will heal when you stop feeling sorry for yourself and think of her problems. Marry her. You can save her the pain she's enduring now.

"Do You have it all figured out how I can do that, God, since she doesn't want me?"

I do. Now you figure it out and marry her.

That stopped Abe. Completely stopped him. How do you marry someone when she tells you in plain words she doesn't love you?

Suddenly, he had a feeling he should take the horses out for a ride. Getting up from the bed, he shoved his hat onto his head, put on his jacket again, and headed for the corral. Both horses greeted him eagerly this time. "Should I saddle you both or ride you, Charity, and lead Sampson?" The horses both danced eagerly and followed him on the other side of the fence until he went into the room referred to as the tack room. He saddled both horses, hopped up into Charity's saddle, and, with Sampson's reins in his left hand, headed west. He'd just give them a little run before it got dark.

Before he realized it, he found himself approaching Martha's covered wagon. He started to rein Charity south but then he thought, why not, and moved up to the wagon and stopped the horses. "Anyone home?" he called. "Quiet," he said softly to the eagerly prancing horses who weren't ready to stop.

Her dark head appeared between the dirty white